MORE THAN WE IMAGINE

A Novel

by
E. G. Brook

ISBN 978-1-7782052-1-7

To Wendy and Greg & Mary and Wayne
My love and appreciation for the caring generosity
of "home"

Chapter 1

It was barely past sunrise, and the morning was blanketed with heat. Amelia stood resolutely on the dusty dirt road, an older woman in cotton shirt and capris, not likely to attract the attention of any passerby. The breeze blew wisps of her long hair about her face, as it had all those younger years of her life. Attention had been easily won, and easily accepted. Not anymore, which was partly her choosing. With clear, steady green eyes she gazed across the yellowed baseball field to the castles, a row of old white houses flanked by orchard. The field grass was so dry she could smell the parched dirt beneath it. The deep, heavy scent reminded her of burden, of loss. A heat wave could be merciless. Change could be the greatest challenge.

"Good morning Amelia," George said, the affection in his familiar voice bringing her back from reflection. She instinctively turned in his direction, welcomed by his blue eyes smiling beneath a Panama hat. He stood close by, his arms full of paper grocery bags. He was fit for a middle-aged man, a quality she attributed to his work and lifestyle.

"It's so hot and dry I can smell the dirt," she said, bridging her thoughts to his presence.

"Mmm," he murmured, noticing her frown. He asked the inevitable question, "Are you worried about the fruit crops?"

"Not yet," she replied, silently acknowledging worry was pressing in on her. She was determined to stay free of it.

Amelia had lived her life in British Columbia, most of it in the Okanagan - the 'place of water' early inhabitants had called the valley. Despite the expansive lake that anchored the area, she rarely noticed a heat moderating affect.

She looked toward the vineyard that stretched across the land on her right, watching the rows of vines emerge from the shadows as the rising sun bathed them in early light. Alessandro had added the café nestled at the vineyard's edge fifteen years ago; now it was a landmark.

Her gaze roamed to the ball field in front of her, and across it to the cherry orchard just beyond the castles. Shadow and sunlight moved through the trees, and in the quiet of the morning she could hear sprinklers pulse the rhythm of a thirsty summer.

"Going over to the castles?" George asked. He seemed to know the right moment to interrupt her thoughts.

"I am," she responded with a slight smile, turning back to him. "I'm going to check on Nicia."

"Good," he said, rebalancing the two grocery bags he held in each arm, shifting one toward her. "Help me with this? It's for Nicia."

"Sure," she agreed, taking the bag. George's characteristic generosity lightened her mood and she stepped onto the baseball field with him, heading toward the castles.

The ball field was bordered by the dirt road that ran the length of the café vineyard, curved and ran in front of Amelia's house. It stretched to the castles and cherry orchard on the far side, and the remaining side was lined with bleachers. Behind the bleachers the field butted up to the elementary school playground and subdivision housing. Amelia glanced toward the houses as they walked, thinking she might see some of the neighborhood children she knew.

There were no early risers outdoors.

"I think it's too hot for Nicia," George mentioned, "but she won't admit it. I tell her to drink lots, keep her skin damp or soak her feet in cool water. I don't think she does."

"She's 80 George. I imagine by that age a woman gets tired of doing what someone is telling her to."

He chuckled. "No matter, we all have to deal with this heat."

She glanced over at him, handsome and weathered under his hat. He'd travelled and worked overseas for close to twenty years, more than half of it in Australia. A man of the world, everyone had said when he'd left their small town right after high school. They'd believed he'd never be back to settle.

"We aren't all as adaptable as a man of the world," Amelia teased.

"Man of the world," he scoffed, "man of the 50 cent come back."

"I thought you'd come back with a dollar," she quipped. He chuckled.

His expression grew serious. "It broke another record for June yesterday. That's got to be tough on Ted and everyone working in the orchards. For Ricco too, and his crews in the vineyards."

"They'll let me know if they need to make changes," she assured him. "It's early enough to catch them before they head out, please let them know I'm at Nicia's." He nodded.

They'd reached the castles, the row of plain one-and-a-half storey houses that bordered the field. All seven were painted white with no fence between them, yet each was distinguished by a character created by those who lived inside. Pots of red geraniums welcomed visitors to Nicia's. Amelia stepped into the shade on Nicia's walkway, cast by one of the large maples grown from the saplings her grandfather had planted between the houses. She turned to George; he anticipated her question.

"I'll meet you here after I've seen the others," he told her.

"Okay," she said, smiling again. He had that effect on her.

George smiled and moved on. Amelia paused before going inside, scanning the front of the houses for any sign of something needing repair, a habit she'd developed soon after she began managing the orchards.

The residents of the castles were the employees, and retired employees of Quinn Orchards, a family business Amelia's grandfather had envisioned in the early 1900s. He'd planted the first trees in 1914, just before the war broke out. The castles had been built for workers after the Second World War, and Nicia and her husband had lived there as long as Amelia could remember. Nicia was like family, her caring heart and listening ear had provided a haven for Amelia countless times when she was growing up, often while Nicia baked or prepared a meal. She could still be counted on for frank and loving counsel.

She walked to Nicia's door and knocked loudly before opening it and stepping into the comforting familiarity of the over-furnished living room. "Nicia, it's Amelia," she called, placing the bag of groceries in a well-worn chair and evaluating the feel of the room. It was too warm for so early in the day.

The small Italian woman came in from the kitchen, sweeping short white hair away from her face with a flour dusted hand, brown eyes vibrant as she greeted Amelia. "Hello," she said with her light Italian accent. "I was just about to bake some cookies, but it can wait."

Amelia gave her a hug before she was ushered to the couch, Nicia sitting beside her. "It's hot for baking Nicia," she said. "It didn't cool down much overnight." Amelia fanned herself with her hand, emphasizing the point.

Nicia smiled and caught Amelia's hand, holding it in her lap. "It's early," she stated, dismissing the concern. "It's not hot yet. There's a young family staying next door with Sam, a couple with a new baby. I want to welcome them right. *Torcetti*."

"They'll love it," Amelia agreed. She was an avid fan of Nicia's baking.

"We need to help each other Amelia, you know this. Sam's a generous man. He's opened his home to his great-nephew and family so they have a place to stay. His nephew has work in the orchards, but prices for rent are so high. It's a crime," she stated unequivocally, "there's no question of that. People should be able to afford a home."

Amelia nodded acknowledgment, persevering with her attempt to discover Nicia's condition. "And how are you in your home Nicia, are you continuing to feel well? This extreme heat has been with us for so many days now."

Nicia patted Amelia's hand. "No need to worry about me, I know what to do. I grew up in southern Italy, before we came here. It was *hot* there, hotter than it used to be here." She shrugged a little. "Now it's more the same. I learned as a child, I'll be fine."

Amelia persisted. "George is worried you aren't drinking enough water and keeping yourself cool."

"Oh, George," Nicia chuckled, "he worries too much. Ricco says I should go to the café afternoons when it's so hot, Lucianna will come and get me. I may do that." She studied Amelia for a moment. "You take care of yourself Amelia," she admonished, "you look tired. Keep yourself well as you want to keep us well. It's the only way."

Amelia smiled. "I know," she said, "and I do. Dreams have been waking me up."

"Dreams? Maybe something new coming into your life."

"I don't know about that. They're in the past when my

grandfather was a young man."

"Don't you worry about them, if important the meaning will become clear in time. You carry on to see the others now," Nicia stated, standing up. "I'll carry on with my baking."

Amelia stood as suggested, walking over to the bag of groceries, lifting and handing it to Nicia. "George sent these for you."

Nicia took the bag with a grateful sigh. "That George," she said affectionately, "he's a kind and generous man."

"He is," Amelia agreed, lightly rubbing Nicia's back in a goodbye caress.

She stepped outside into the bright sunlight, pausing on the doorstep, the hot air feeling uncomfortably close on her neck. George was headed toward her, arms free of grocery bags. She took a stretchy hair band from her pocket, swept her hair back and up off her shoulders into a ponytail, wrapping the band tightly around it close to her head, and letting the length fall. George had stopped nearby and was watching with a slight smile. She felt self-conscious with his attention; something about his smile.

"It gets too hot on my neck," she said simply, diffusing her feelings by glancing away from him as she stepped onto the road. He joined her and they walked toward the field. "Who have you seen?"

"Everyone but Jack," George replied, without detail, which was another characteristic of his. Amelia smiled to herself, knowing she would probably have to ask him. They walked on in silence until Amelia turned to him in amusement.

"Are you going to tell me how they're doing?" she prompted as they crossed the expanse of parched grass. He responded as if there'd been no delay.

"Joe and Sarah are okay, sleeping nights on the back

porch. They're helping Merle and Emma with the vegetable garden, which is suffering in the heat, so they've rigged up a tarp for some shade in the afternoon. Ted said he's not worrying about the heat, he's too busy in the orchards dealing with it. He mentioned Jack's COPD is giving him trouble."

"That's not good news," Amelia said with concern.

"At least he stopped smoking over the winter, but I don't know how much it will help. He was sleeping, I didn't disturb him. Ricco, Lucianna and their whole family are in the vineyard and café everyday Ricco said, and they've now got an air conditioning unit in the café, which you know because you had it installed. Sam has his great-nephew Phil and family staying with him, which Nicia probably told you. Phil's working with Ted. Sam's still going to the vineyard to work with Ricco occasionally, and spends afternoons in the café. He told me Nicia's over visiting regularly."

Amelia grinned, wondering how someone who often said so little could summarize that much information.

"What are you grinning at?" George asked, her amusement causing him to grin himself.

Their years of friendship had taught her not to comment, and she side-stepped his question. "Nicia mentioned visiting Sam's," she said. "She was baking Torcetti for Phil and his wife."

"Baking?"

"Baking." Amelia chuckled, turning to George. "She seems to be managing the heat better than we thought. She mentioned Ricco's encouraging her to go to the café during the afternoon."

"Joe told me Lucianna has encouraged him and Sarah to go over to the café and keep cool as well," George said. "I'll drop by to see Jack at lunch, maybe I can get him to go to the café with me."

"I think he will, you're close to him."

George looked at the ground as he walked, remembering. "He's been like a dad to me since I was a kid, and thank God for that. He taught me a lot of things when I was hanging around the castles with Michael. He was always there for me. When Michael died and my mom didn't know how to handle it, Jack kept me occupied."

Amelia felt the familiar ache in her chest with mention of her brother's death. Despite the years since his passing and all she'd learned to help her accept it, there were still times when pain and sorrow swept in. She reminded herself to breathe deeply, to allow it to be, and allow it to pass. Memories came as the ache eased.

"I think Jack understood Michael's gentleness in a way my father never could," she confided, watching George, knowing he'd shut down his feelings about Michael's death.

"He did," George acknowledged quietly, raising his head.

"I've often wished my father had accepted people as they were, instead of seeing them fall short of how he wanted them to be."

George walked on silently for a moment, finally acknowledging, "Michael felt that way too."

They reached the edge of the field and crossed the dirt road, stopping at the wide driveway into Amelia's yard with the gate that was always open. "Ricco mentioned Will Trumble," George said with concern, bringing them back to the present. "Will's talking around town about tearing down the houses and building apartment complexes."

"I've heard."

"Do you think your cousin will sell him the land?"

Amelia smiled wryly. "Mr. Trumble will have a hard time achieving that," she stated and walked into her yard.

"Good. I'm off to work," George announced. He started down the road and turned back to her, issuing a mock order.

"Stay cool Amelia."

She saluted, shook her shirt loose and started up the driveway to the family home she'd inherited and loved. Her grandfather had built the house in 1925, hiring craftsmen whose promise was "everlasting" – a description that had become a family endearment. She and Alessandro had updated the interior when the house had come to her, improving livability for their family's needs, yet ensuring character was kept. Still, it was the wrap-around porch that Amelia cherished most, the place of happy summer evenings spent with family and friends throughout her life. It was one of the few places she could remember sharing quiet times with her father, times her grandfather had encouraged her to guard well.

She stopped by a wilting rose bush as she neared the stairs to the porch, examining the leaves to ensure the cause was only the heat. A vehicle pulled into the driveway, and Amelia turned to see a noticeably clean truck park directly in front of the stairs. Will Trumble climbed out, a tall, slim man in his mid-30s. He stood waiting for her, spotlessly dressed in pressed linen pants and an unwrinkled polo shirt. Will had grown into the man she imagined he would when she'd known him as a boy; bold but anxious. He and her son had been friends all through school, and Will had a tendency to outreach himself. He nervously swept his fair hair back from his brow and shifted his weight from one foot to the other as she walked toward him.

"Good morning Will," she said with a knowing tone as she drew near him. "It's early for a business call."

"Good morning Mrs. Marin, I hope you're well," he said, pausing awkwardly as he searched for words to explain the early hour. "It's best to get things done early in this heat."

"We can agree on that," she stated as she walked past him and around the truck, climbing up the stairs to the front porch. He slowly followed her. "It must be important business to warrant the formality of Mrs. Marin," she said and turned to him, his blue eyes averted as they often were when he was directly spoken to. She wanted to establish her ground, and at the same time put him at ease. "You're an adult now Will, feel free to call me Amelia," she suggested, and motioned toward a wicker chair. "Sit down a moment. Tell me what's on your mind."

"Thank you, but it wouldn't feel right to call you by your first name," he said, glancing at her. "I'll come straight to business Mrs. Marin. I've got a plan to build on the land where the old houses are by the ball field. I could fit two apartment buildings side by side there, each three stories high, the maximum height allowed by the town. I've casually mentioned the idea to some of the town Council members, and interest is favorable. I'd like to contact your family in Ontario with an offer to buy the land."

"What do you know about those houses Will?" she asked.

He was hesitant to answer, and seemed slightly embarrassed. "What everyone does I guess, they're not slums but pretty run down. People live there who can't afford to live anywhere else. It would be good for the town to improve on them."

"What do you have in mind for the people who live there?"

"Well they'd have to relocate naturally."

"Where to?"

Will looked perplexed. "Where they choose to I'm sure."

"Are you Will? I'm not sure at all."

"I don't understand."

"That seems obvious," she stated as she stood up, signifying the meeting was over. "Perhaps you'd like some time to think about it."

Will stood up, looking confused.

Amelia walked toward her front door, feeling sadness behind her irritation. Despite what she knew of Will, she'd hoped he would have more understanding. She turned squarely to him as she reached the door. "Those houses were built to provide homes for workers who helped us on our land. They've been well maintained for three generations by my family," she stated, opened the door and stepped inside. "Goodbye Mr. Trumble. Be prosperous with your day."

Will stood stupefied for a moment. He turned and quickly descended the stairs, getting into his truck and driving away.

* * *

It was still early when George steered his truck into a parking spot outside the Municipal Centre. He strode into the single storey air conditioned building, welcoming the coolness he could enjoy for a brief time before heading to work in the parks. Town offices were a little cramped in the building, but it made communications between departments easy. It also made keeping conversations private a problem. He passed the Planning and Development department on the way to his Parks and Recreation office, and noticed Will Trumble was there talking with Steve. He could hear them as he tossed his hat on a shelf and manoeuvered around his desk to sit down. He thought he should block it out, and turned on his computer. His second thought was it might be important to know what they were saying. He settled in and listened, Will's voice had his attention.

"That's what she said," Will emphasized, sitting rigidly across from Steve. "She basically told me to go away and think about it."

"So what are you going to do?" Steve asked, leaning back in his chair. His patience with process was well developed as the third generation of the Hayashi family living in the valley. Will's wasn't. His parents had moved in when Will was nine, and a rural lifestyle had never been a good fit for him.

Will dismissively waved the question aside. "Isn't there anyway I can get the contact for her relatives without going through her? It must be listed somewhere."

"She's the contact listed on all the documents I've seen," Steve replied. "The title is A.J. Quinn, contact Amelia Marin, manager."

"Well I can't put the plan through for approval without owning the land," Will stated, exasperated. "Can we make it a community improvement issue, getting rid of those old houses? Would Council go for that?"

"No one's complaining about them," Steve said.

"But they're right next to the new school and subdivision," Will declared, restlessly standing up and pacing the few steps in front of Steve's desk. "All that's been built within the last 10 years. The ball field's been developed, the whole area's been developed except those old houses," Will stated emphatically.

"You got in on some of that building if I remember correctly," Steve noted.

"Exactly," Will acknowledged, missing Steve's point. "That's why I want to carry it over to development where those houses sit."

"Not likely Council's going to go for it as a community issue Will," Steve stated calmly. "The land for the school and subdivision was donated by A. J. Quinn and rezoned by special approval. Amelia Marin was instrumental in the process. She's thought pretty well of, and those houses are on her family's land. They'll stay there if she says so. Look somewhere else for your project."

"I've looked," Will said, putting his hands on Steve's desk and leaning forward with frustration. "There's no land that suits the project as well as that piece, and anything close would involve rezoning, also not likely to get."

"This is an agricultural area," Steve stated frankly. "That's how it is."

"Well I'm not giving up," Will insisted, abruptly leaving the office.

George leaned back in his chair as he heard Will leave, wondering why the build mattered so much to him.

* * *

Amelia moved about her kitchen a little restlessly, pouring herself a drink of water from a covered pitcher on the island counter. She stood staring out the window for a moment, then walked over and sat at the table. She sipped from the glass and gazed past the garden to the white houses in the distance. "They're castles," she said quietly, "not old houses."

She remembered when Michael had given the worker's cottages the name. It had been a late spring day with the orchards in bloom, the air warm and fragrant, a time of year she and Michael loved. Her mother had sent them to get their father for lunch. There was no ball field then, only an open field of grass with a few wildflowers. Michael was only five and she was 12, so she'd let him race ahead of her. He'd stopped triumphantly as he'd reached the dirt road by the houses, laughed as he'd looked back at her and thrown up his arms in victory.

"I beat you!"

"You did!" she'd called out, and ran to catch up to him. She'd hugged him close and he'd squirmed and jumped as he laughed. They'd heard the bang of an old screen door close, and had turned to see a younger Nicia come onto the front walkway by her house, just as her husband had crossed the road from the orchard.

"Was just coming to get you," she'd called to him. "Lunch

is on the table." She'd noticed them as she turned to go back into the house, and waved. They'd waved back.

"She's a nice lady," Michael had said. "I'm glad she has a castle."

"What do you mean, a castle?" Amelia had asked, puzzled.

"Her home. Dad said a man's home is his castle. It must be the same for a woman too," he'd insisted, turning to her earnestly, "don't you think Amelia? She doesn't have much else. The kids at school say so."

Amelia had put her hand on his back affectionately as they'd turned toward the orchard. "You've got a kind heart Michael."

Her cell phone rang, bringing Amelia back to the present, back from missing Michael. She rose and crossed to the counter, picking up the phone and checking the screen. With a delighted smile she set it on speaker and answered the call.

"Lucca! How wonderful to hear from you."

"Hi Mom, how are you doing in the heat?" he asked in his usual breezy manner.

"I'm fine, keeping cool as I can."

"Tell me you're not working in the orchards," he joked, though his tone held her to account.

Amelia laughed. "I'm not working in the orchards," she said, "and so far everything's okay."

"I've been thinking I would come up for a while and help Ricco in the vineyards."

"Can you get time off work?"

"Not a problem, we're between projects and I've got lots of overtime logged."

"Maybe you need a break Lucca, not more work," Amelia said with a little concern.

"No, no. I don't want to be awake nights hearing Dad's voice in my head," he insisted, playfully adopting his father's Italian accent as he continued, "'*Lucca you should take more interest in the land.'"*

Amelia sensed a residual tension behind Lucca's teasing. "Your father was proud of you becoming an engineer, you know that," she assured him, distractedly folding the edge of a napkin on the counter. Lucca was silent. She felt uncomfortable herself, and hoped Lucca would accept her assurance. Alessandro had been proud. "Of course come," she consented warmly. "I'd love to see you, and there's no doubt Ricco will be grateful for your help. Be prepared for the heat, you've got a buffer down there on the coast."

"This is not my first rodeo Mom," Lucca said, amused.

She chuckled, but spoke seriously. "I know we've had heat spikes before Lucca, but this is different. It's intense and it's lasting."

There was brief silence before Lucca spoke. "Then it's good I'm coming," he said decisively. "I'm flying in this afternoon, Will's picking me up."

"Will?" she echoed with surprise.

"Yeah, we're going to catch up while I'm there. I'm hoping to spend some time at the lake with him."

"You'll be here for dinner?"

"Definitely. See you around six."

"Looking forward to it," she said. "'Bye, travel safe."

"'Bye Mom."

Amelia put the phone in her pocket and finished drinking the glass of water, curious about Lucca connecting with Will. She hadn't realized they'd kept in touch, and wondered if wanting to make the land purchase would come up between them. Maybe it already had, she considered as she placed the glass in the sink. She grabbed a muffin from a basket on the island, and crossed to pick up her hat from the table on her way outside. Speculation wasn't going to help her.

Outdoors was Amelia's favorite place to be, and had been for as long as she could remember. When she was a child it often meant time spent in the orchards helping out, and after marrying it also included working with Alessandro in the vineyards. She'd balanced the work with swimming, following the pattern of her childhood summers. Her mother had taken her to the lake every day, with Michael when he came along. She'd kept that tradition when her own children were growing up.

Over the last two years she'd made an effort to develop new outdoor activities. She had more available time on her hands since she'd given Ted a greater role in managing the orchards with her. The shift had been an uneasy one, yet now the time and attention she gave to her yard and garden was a pleasure. Though her flower beds weren't extensive, it was challenging to keep the plants thriving in the heat.

Her present focus was on the wilting yellow rose bush. She set the water jug she carried on the ground, and knelt to finger the soil at the base of the rose. It was no surprise to find it bone dry in her hand. With a sigh she swept a strand of hair from her face, lifted the jug and poured a flow of water over the loose, dry dirt. Her cell phone rang and she pulled it from her pocket, habitually checking the screen before answering the call.

"Hi Ted," she said, and listened intently with the phone to her ear. She stood up and began to pace. "Do you think the fruit is getting burnt?" She stood still, listening to his response, feeling her body tense. "I'll come down," she stated, deliberately keeping her voice even. "I know. I understand Ted, we've got enough water." She completed the call and immediately headed toward the cherry orchard across from the castles.

Chapter 2

Ted was a lean, muscular man in his late forties, and met her by the outdoor tap embedded in a post at the edge of the orchard. A fringe of brown hair stuck to his damp forehead under a canvas hat, his shirt clung to his heavily perspiring body. He held a handful of shrivelled, discolored cherries toward her.

Amelia took the cherries apprehensively. They felt slightly sticky and dry in her hands. "They almost look dehydrated," she observed. "Is this top of the tree or lower too?"

"I've only seen it top on a few. We've got a lot of checking to do through all the trees. Like I said on the phone, we're changing the irrigation to one hour time blocks and shifting throughout the orchard. If we can rotate through and keep everything damp, that and evaporation might help cool things a bit."

"What about the other orchards?"

"We've lost some fruit in all of them. I don't know how much yet," Ted said, maintaining his remedial approach. "I think there's less apricot and peach damage than in the cherry orchards. Some apples have brown spots. It's almost like they cook on the branch."

Amelia was shocked. "I've never seen anything like this," she said, looking over the orchard.

"We've never been this hot before."

"Are the trees being damaged too?"

Ted looked at her, his dark eyes full of concern. "I can't say about that yet," he admitted. He pulled a cotton kerchief from his pocket and took off his hat, wiping his face and sweeping his hair back before putting the hat back on. "If you agree we'll follow the same irrigation pattern everywhere," he stated, watching for her approval.

She met his gaze, then looked away to the orchard in an attempt to hide the pained expression she felt rising in her face. "I appreciate what you're doing Ted," she said. "Go ahead with changing irrigation in the other orchards as well. Please keep me updated as all the cherry orchards are checked, and make sure the crew do a thorough job." She took another look at the shrivelled cherries in her hand and shoved them in her pocket. She turned back to Ted, composed. "We'll get through it okay," she assured him.

He nodded his acknowledgement, and headed toward several workers examining cherries on nearby trees. Amelia stared after him a moment, stunned by news of what was occurring. With methodical practicality she took a cotton scarf from her pocket and bent down to the tap, turning it on and soaking the scarf. She left it dripping and wiped over the exposed skin on her arms and legs, then wet it again and stood up, tying it loosely around her neck. Water trickled down over her, helping to ease her tension as she lifted her shirt away from where it clung to her. She headed back across the ball field, pulling the phone from her pocket as she walked. She called Ricco and set the call on speaker.

Ricco answered gravely, "Hello Amelia. I was planning to speak with you today."

A wave of anguish swept over her with his words. She stopped, closing her eyes and speaking with deliberate calm. "How are the grapes Ricco?"

"No problem there," he said, "so far no damage."

"In all vineyards?"

"Yes, all are fine."

She smiled with relief, opening her eyes and walking on as Ricco spoke.

"I've lost two workers," he said. "Guys from the coast, it's too hot for them."

She stopped at her driveway. "Can you replace them?"

"Yes, but they're young," he answered. "My youngest daughter and my sister's son, both 13. They want to learn. Otherwise I could start looking, but I don't know how long it would take."

She hesitated, her eyes fixed on the café vineyard at the base of the hillside. "Hire your daughter and nephew Ricco," she decided. "Teach them."

"We'll be okay then," he said. "We can manage."

"Lucca's arriving tonight to help in the vineyards for a while," she told him.

"Good!" Ricco exclaimed.

"Good," she echoed in agreement, and completed the call. She continued to look toward the vineyard, wiping perspiration from her face with the back of her hand. It wasn't yet noon and the heat was oppressive. She wondered about Nicia and the others going to the café to get out of the heat, and hoped they did.

* * *

George held the wooden door of Alessandro's café open for Jack to shuffle inside. The old man's wheezing prompted George to keep a protective, steadying arm near him. Jack's condition had changed dramatically, and George wasn't sure how to handle it.

"Let's sit over here," George said, steering Jack toward a table next to the windows. Jack's faded cotton work clothes hung loosely on his solid frame as he moved slowly toward the table and sat down with a grateful sigh, followed by a rattling cough. His complexion had a grey hue beneath the flush from effort, his blue eyes watered. George's anxiousness was growing; he needed to know how to help Jack, and was afraid he couldn't.

"Not so hot in here," Jack said in gasping breaths.

"I hope it helps you feel better. Amelia made a good choice installing air conditioning," George acknowledged, removing his hat and tossing it on a spare chair. Jack nodded his agreement. "She's made a lot of good choices in here," George added, looking around, distracting himself from the sensations he felt building in his chest.

Amelia's touch was everywhere in the earthen-winery décor of the café. The large room was filled with small wooden tables and chairs arranged among large plants, creating a feeling of comfort and privacy wherever you sat. The rows of ceiling fans were still, and the air cooled by the new unit was obviously pleasing many customers seated throughout the café. A row of windows overlooked the vineyard, and glass doors led to an open air terrace with tables noticeably empty in the heat.

Jack convulsed in a coughing spell, holding a kerchief to his mouth. George fought to suppress an urge to hold him. He raised his hand, attempting to catch Lucianna's attention as she served guests with her full-bodied vitality. She didn't notice. George looked to Aria emulating her mother's friendly manner nearby, but she was turned away from him. Intent on keeping occupied and getting service, he looked for Lucianna and Ricco's daughter-in-law Capriana. He spotted her across the room, carrying full plates of food to a couple. He raised his hand, waving persistently. Capriana nodded, acknowledging his signal with a smile.

Relieved, George sat back and glanced to Jack wearily

E.G. Brook

leaning against the back of his chair, his eyes closed. He coughed again, then with several gasps brought his breath to a wheezing rest. George felt helpless. He looked for Capriana and saw she was heading his way, fastening a strand of dark hair under a decorative clasp. A man stopped her, and she paused courteously to answer his question. Frustrated, George turned back to the table. Jack was watching him, breathing more easily. George recognized the look.

"Hungry Jack?" he asked, wanting to divert him. He knew where the conversation was going.

Jack shrugged slightly. "A little," he replied, steadily staring. George couldn't look away. "You've got to face it," Jack said in gasping breaths. "Long overdue."

George knew Jack was referring to Michael's death, and his denial of how it had affected him. He'd avoided yielding to Jack's guidance about death all these years, no matter how much he needed and wanted it. It was a stubbornness he couldn't budge; a holding-out aversion to the pain he was sure was behind the fear.

Jack held his gaze steadily on George's face. "You know," he wheezed.

Despite Jack's physical weakness, George could feel his spirit with him as strongly as he ever had; love was undeniable. Desperate to have a choice other than the one Jack was calling him to, George looked away. He couldn't face losing him.

Joe and Sarah's laughter rang across the café and George turned, spotting his elderly Indigenous friends seated with Nicia at a corner table. Nicia was chatting with a fair-haired young woman who held a sleeping baby in her arms. Phil's wife Hannah, George imagined. Nicia could easily make a newcomer feel welcome.

"Nicia's here," he pointed out to Jack. "We could stop by the table after we eat," he suggested. The challenge was gone from Jack's eyes, and he looked toward Nicia's table with a weak smile, nodding in agreement.

Lucianna came to the table and filled their glasses with ice water, smiling at George and turning her attention to Jack, her dark eyes expressively affectionate. "So good to see you here Jack," she said warmly, with the slight Italian lilt of her voice. "We're happy you came."

Jack smiled at her. "Will Ricco be by?" he wheezed.

"Yes, he could be here anytime now," she answered, adding with emphasis, "I tell him to get out of the hottest part of the day too."

Jack laughed and coughed a little. "I like to hear how things are in the vineyard," he said, "and Ricco's gone before I'm up these days."

Lucianna nodded understanding. "Hard to leave behind, eh Jack? You were many years at Ricco's side. You got him started," she acknowledged. "What would you like?" she asked, looking at both of them. "Shall I bring you our special today? Risotto, salami, light salad."

Both men nodded yes. "Thanks Lucianna," George said and relaxed, leaning back in his chair. Lucianna smiled and walked toward the kitchen. He realized how tired he was feeling and told himself it was the late lunch, not wanting to attribute anything to Jack's condition, or admit the heat was getting to him. The clock on the wall read 2:15. Today, like the last few days, he'd been working in full sun clearing debris at the hillside parks. He ran his hand through his hair and sighed. It hadn't seemed like debris before this heat, but now the risk of fire was on everyone's minds.

George noticed Will Trumble enter the café, accompanied by a dark-skinned man over dressed for the heat. He didn't recognize him, but the suit suggested the man was from out of town. George watched intently as the two crossed to a table on the far side of the room. They'd barely sat down before they were engrossed in conversation.

"George. Jack!" Ricco's voice drew his attention back toward the door. Ricco was striding toward them in his worn cotton work clothes, straw hat in hand. Sam, Emma and Merle were following him, with Sam looking the sturdiest of them all, weaving through the tables in his loose, sweaty work clothes, canvas hat still on his head. Emma's long brown hair was damp about her face, and the length hung limply over her usual cotton dress. Merle was in shorts and a t-shirt, his Metis heritage clear in his features, his dark hair tied back. They all looked exhausted as they sat at the next table. Ricco leaned back, wiping his brow with a kerchief. "Good to see you both here," he said. "Glad you came Jack," he emphasized. "You've come to check up on me, haven't you?" he teased.

Jack shrugged a little and smiled.

"The grapes are fine," Ricco assured him, leaning over and patting him on the back. "We're okay," he sighed.

Lucianna arrived with the food for George and Jack, setting plates down in front of them.

"Lucianna," George asked, leaning forward, "have you seen that man with Will Trumble before?"

Lucianna looked in Will's direction, then back to George. "He was in for dinner last night," she said. "Will was with him then too. I heard him mention real estate opportunities around here. I think Will mentioned Amelia."

"Thanks," said George, briefly watching the two men in conversation. He turned to his meal, setting all thoughts of Will, clearing parks and intense heat aside.

* * *

Amelia's backyard was still and quiet, the heat of late afternoon had caused all living things to seek refuge. Her exposed skin was damp from the tepid water she'd sponged over it, and she lay resting in the hammock under the large shade trees, relatively comfortable in a cotton dress, hat by her side. She had prepared what she thought Lucca would like for dinner, and with eyes closed she practiced what she'd learned so many years ago, wanting to shift her worry about the orchards to acceptance. With each breath she inhaled more deeply, and exhaled more fully. She began to feel drowsy, soothed by the sound of water trickling over stones in the nearby fountain.

"You look peaceful," George said quietly.

"George!" she exclaimed with an involuntary gasp, her eyes flashing open.

He smiled apologetically, a little amused. "Sorry, I didn't mean to startle you. You just looked so peaceful."

"That was my intention," she said and smiled forgivingly. She raised her hand to shade her eyes against the brightness behind him. "You, on the other hand, look worried."

George shrugged. "Work. Fire risk."

"Pull up a seat," she said, motioning toward a lawn chair.

"No, dusty from work. I'll sit on the ground." He sank down onto the grass beside her, taking a kerchief from his pocket and wiping perspiration from his face.

"Can I get you a drink of something cool?" she asked.

"No, don't get up."

She was quiet a moment, feeling his tension, sensing something was on his mind. George stuffed the kerchief back in his pocket and gazed over toward the castles.

"Spill it George."

He smiled slightly, turning back to her. "I saw Will at the café this afternoon."

She remained silent, waiting. That wasn't all that was bothering him.

"He was with someone I haven't seen around here before, a guy in a suit."

"I can see how that would worry you," Amelia quipped.

He chuckled. "I asked Lucianna about him, and she said he'd been there for dinner last night with Will. They were talking real estate, and your name was mentioned."

"Did she have more to add to that?" Amelia asked.

George shook his head no. Amelia swung her legs over the edge of the hammock and climbed out of it, realizing he wasn't going to say more.

"No worries there, Will's just trying to get his way," she said and motioned toward the hammock. "Lie down and relax," she encouraged him. "Listen to the fountain, it works wonders."

"Not now," he said and stood up, looking toward the fountain. "Doesn't it use a lot of water?"

"Not at all, the pump recycles it."

"Hmm," he murmured. "Clever."

"I got the idea from a land with little water and much food," she said, but before she could elaborate she heard a truck in the driveway.

"Lucca!" she exclaimed, and hurried around the house to meet him.

Will's truck was pulling out of the driveway as she reached the front walkway. Lucca was standing by the steps looking relaxed in linen pants and blue shirt, his suitcase beside him. He grinned at her with a smile that reflected his father, along with his dark hair and vibrant brown eyes. She hugged him close. "You look like you never get outside," she playfully observed, standing back and turning him around, which he agreeably allowed. "At least you're wearing something good for the heat."

"I've been here seconds," he teased, "and you're acting like a mom."

"I am a mom," she acknowledged, and laughed. "Come on, let's go inside," she said enthusiastically, starting up the stairs. "I've got a light meal ready. We can eat more when it's cooler if you like."

"I've hardly noticed the heat," Lucca said, walking with her. "And it is hot at the coast too. I've been in air conditioning constantly."

"George," Amelia called to him as he reached the walkway below them. "Come in and have dinner with us."

"Hey George," Lucca called. "Good to see you."

"Hi Lucca," George responded, hesitating briefly before he grinned and took off his hat.

"Sounds good to me," he said as he climbed the stairs. "Lucca can fill me in on the fame and fortune of a world class engineer."

"Not a chance," Lucca joked. "Trade secrets."

George chuckled and tossed his hat on the small coffee table in the midst of the wicker furniture on the porch.

Lucca followed Amelia into the house and glanced around. "Looks the same," he mentioned, then noticed the ceiling fans whirring above them. "Mom," he said incredulously, "you don't have air conditioning yet?"

Amelia laughed. "I've always liked the heat," she said, "until now." She moved quickly through the living room to the kitchen, fanning herself with her hat. "I'm undecided about making the change," she stated.

With an air of purpose she dropped the hat on the island counter, washed her hands at the sink, grabbed a paper towel to dry them and opened the fridge. She moved two covered bowls to the island counter and went back for a pitcher of iced tea. George came into the kitchen as she got glasses and plates from the cupboard and took them to the table.

"Have a seat," she said to him, uncovering the bowls and systematically moving everything over to the table. George watched her with amusement.

"What are you smiling at?" she asked lightly. "We have

dinner together all the time."

"You're so excited," he noted, seating himself.

"I am," she agreed enthusiastically, crossing to a drawer and getting cutlery. She moved back to the table and set three places, picked up the pitcher and sat opposite George. "It's the first time Lucca's been home in years," she said, pouring the iced tea. "We've always visited in the city." She paused, thinking. "Since Alessandro passed," she added. She put the pitcher down, suddenly subdued. "I hadn't realized that connection."

Lucca came into the kitchen. "Bedroom looks the same too," he said, smiling. "I thought you would have made it an office or something by now." He sat down at the side of the table and took a drink of iced tea.

Amelia didn't have a response. George teased, "Don't you know mothers make it their mission to keep things the same?" Amelia looked at him in disbelief. "Except your mother," he quickly added, "who has been intent on changing things most of her life."

"Good save," Amelia said. George grinned. Lucca looked at the two of them curiously.

Amelia motioned to the two bowls. "Antipasto salad and green salad," she said, picking up a bowl and handing it to Lucca, and passing the other to George. "Let's eat now and clean up later. It's cooler on the porch, we can relax out there. Or count dragonflies," she added with a grin, remembering Lucca's childhood pastime.

"With dessert?" questioned Lucca, passing by the dragonfly remark.

"I can manage that," agreed Amelia, chuckling.

They lingered over the meal, hearing about Lucca's last project and the one that was coming up. George talked briefly about the fire risk, Amelia was silent about the fruit loss in the orchards. She encouraged George and Lucca to move out to the porch while she dropped dishes in the sink and got dessert. She soon joined them with three small bowls balanced in her hands.

"Gelato I bet," said Lucca, leaning forward in the wicker chair to take the bowl and spoon she offered. He scooped some into his mouth. "And good!" he said appreciatively. "Is this store bought or Lucianna's?"

"Lucianna's of course," Amelia stated, moving to where George was leaning against the porch railing and handing him a bowl. He smiled his thanks. "She brings me some almost every week," Amelia added, relaxing against the rail next to George, bowl in hand.

Lucca had already finished and placed the empty bowl on the small table between them. He sat back, looking to the sun hovering above the hillside, noticing there were dragonflies flitting in the waning light. He smiled. "The evening doesn't seem to be cooling off much," he observed.

"It's been that way for several nights," Amelia said, "which is putting more stress on the trees."

"I hope it changes soon," George commented, putting his bowl on the table.

Lucca turned his eyes to Amelia. "Mom, have you thought about what will happen with the orchards and vineyards when you retire?"

"Retire?" Amelia echoed with a chuckle. "I'm past retirement age Lucca, I don't think that will ever happen."

"Seriously, when it's too much for you to manage anymore, what do you think you'll do?"

Amelia studied him a moment. "I haven't thought about it very much," she responded honestly.

Lucca attempted to look nonchalant, but she could tell he had something on his mind. "Maybe you should," he suggested.

Amelia put her bowl on the table and looked at him,

E.G. Brook

measuring her words. "Your father wanted you and Julia to have the vineyards and café after I'm gone, you know that. He stated it in his Will."

"I can't see myself doing that," he stated, "and Julia can't either."

"You and Julia have spoken about it?"

"Yes."

"When?"

"Recently."

Amelia was stunned. "I had no idea you wouldn't want what your father left you."

Lucca sat forward. "Mom, it's not like that," he said apologetically.

"What is it like?" she asked evenly. Lucca didn't respond, but sat back in his chair.

"Maybe we should talk about it another time," he said.

"Good idea," Amelia agreed frankly. She'd rather have the conversation when she wasn't upset.

Lucca stood up, wanting to ease the tension. "Let's walk over to the café for a glass of wine."

"We've got wine here," Amelia responded with more irritation in her voice than she was comfortable with.

"But they've got air conditioning," Lucca said, giving her a disarming smile. "Will mentioned it."

"It's about time for me to head home," George said, believing it was best for him to leave. "You two enjoy the stroll."

"There's no need for you to leave George. Lucca, you go ahead. Ricco and Sam will likely be there and happy to see you," Amelia stated. Lucca hesitated. "It's fine," she said with a relaxing breath, finally accepting the situation. "I'm up very early in the morning, it won't be long before I'm in bed."

"You're sure?" Lucca questioned.

"Sure," Amelia emphasized, confident they'd be able to talk it through when the time was right. "We'll catch up tomorrow."

"Okay," he said, and kissed her forehead before heading down the stairs. "'Night Mom, 'bye George."

George moved over to the porch swing and sat down, patting the seat next to him. Amelia sat beside him. He moved the swing slightly back and forth.

"That was completely unexpected," she confided, slumping back in the swing with disappointment.

"Mmm," George murmured.

Amelia abruptly sat forward and turned to him. "You thought it would happen," she said with surprise.

"*Might* happen," George corrected, and put a comforting arm around her shoulders. She kept looking at him. He shrugged. "Lucca was always eager to leave here and get to the city."

"I thought that would change as he got older," she admitted.

"Not all things change Amelia," he said quietly.

Amelia looked out into the night, easing the sorrow she felt with the movement of the swing. It was unfathomable that Lucca and Julia didn't want their inheritance from their father. She could only bear that thought for a moment. She set it aside and brought up a different subject, turning to George.

"I seem to dream more on hot nights," she said with a lightheartedness she hoped the conversation would make real. "Do you dream?"

"I dream," he replied.

"And remember them?"

"When I want to remember them."

She chuckled. "Selective dreaming, imagine that."

"You don't mind remembering them all?"

"No I don't mind," she replied with a youthful pleasure, looking out into the garden. "I kinda' like it. Dreams can take you anywhere."

"That's the trouble."

Amelia turned to him with empathy. "You're troubled by your dreams?" George shrugged casually. "Not anything worth talking about."

"Mmm," she murmured, placing her hand on his back, caressing lightly as she turned back to the garden. "I've been having the same dream on and off, about my grandfather's life in San Francisco before he moved here. At least that's what I think it's about. Not sure."

"Curious," George noted.

"It is," Amelia agreed. "I wonder about it."

He'd relaxed with her touch. She swept her hand across his shoulders and stood up, reaching out to help him from the swing. "Come on, time to call it a day."

George smiled, taking her hand unnecessarily and rising from the swing with ease. He picked up his hat from the table and playfully tipped it to her before putting it on. "Goodnight Amelia," he said, "sweet dreams."

She smiled. "Goodnight George."

Amelia watched him climb into his truck, then went inside and methodically loaded dishes into the dishwasher. The heat was oppressively hovering in the night air, and she wearily ambled down the hallway to her bedroom, sweeping aside thoughts of the day. The ceiling fan turned quietly above her as she went into the bathroom and came out in her cotton nightgown, her hair damp about her face. She removed the band from her hair and let it fall loosely over her shoulders and down her back. More exhausted with the heat than she cared to admit she crawled under the light sheet on her bed, grateful for the comforting support of the mattress beneath her. The soft whirring sound of the fan lulled her into sleep.

The perspiring dampness of her body didn't seem to matter, though she unconsciously wiped her brow with the back of her hand. Images behind closed eyelids signalled her drifting into dreams. Worlds seemingly moved within her.

Lucca was first up in the morning and already in the kitchen when Amelia padded in barefoot, wearing a lightweight robe. He sat at the table, dressed in the same loose cotton work clothes most of the workers wore in the vineyards, and looked very much like his father had for so many years. She found it a little unnerving, bringing memory of Alessandro close to life. Lucca was finishing what looked like a plate of eggs and toast, and had made coffee. Amelia helped herself to coffee and sat opposite him, taking his straw hat from the table and tossing it onto the island. That, too, was like his father.

"Good morning," he said, smiling at her having moved the hat. "How'd you sleep? This seems late for you to be getting going."

She smiled slightly. "Good morning," she said, taking a drink of coffee before answering his question. "It is later than usual," she agreed, looking at him sleepily. "A dream woke me in the middle of the night. I couldn't get back to sleep for hours."

"Good dream, bad dream?" he asked.

"I'm not sure," she said, feeling a little wary of deciding.

"Tell me about it," Lucca urged her, curious about what had kept her awake.

"I've been having this dream for a while now. I'm with my grandfather, but he's a young man around 18. I'm about 12. We're in San Francisco in the early 1900s, when he lived there. He takes me into a large room crowded with men in suits, and even more women in long dresses and hats. We listen to an elderly white haired man speak, but I can't understand what he's saying. We leave, and there's a little

E.G. Brook

dark-haired girl waiting for us on the street. My grandfather leaves me and goes to her, takes her hand and very affectionately says her name, Grace."

"Nice name," Lucca commented, sipping his coffee.

Amelia started, having an intuitive sense the dream had something to do with Lucca, but she couldn't determine how.

Lucca watched her with a quizzical expression. "Is that it?"

"No," she said. "My grandfather and Grace begin to walk away, and I try to call out but I can't speak; my voice is held back. They walk out of sight, and I jolt awake." With a tiny shudder she turned toward the window, reliving the vividness of the dream, the feeling of her grandfather leaving her. "It feels very real."

"You're left alone," Lucca acknowledged with compassion. "There's got to be something associated with that."

Amelia sipped her coffee. "There's a lot associated with that," she admitted, and said nothing more.

"How well did you know your grandfather?"

"I was very close to him." Her mood lightened with the memory of her grandfather as she knew him. "I thought he was really old, though he must have only been in his 70s when I was little," she said, reminiscing. "He had a kinder way about him than my father, I loved to be with him. He often read to me when I was really young, and took me into the orchards as I got older. He taught me everything about the trees, and told me about his fruit trees in San Francisco. I remember the trouble he had with pests there, he was so adamant when he talked about it," she stated with a slight smile. "He was happy most of the time, often encouraging people to change things for the better." She lifted her hair back from her face, relaxed and leaned her elbow on the table, resting her head in her hand as she looked at Lucca.

"My father didn't agree with him about change, but I think I picked it up from him."

Lucca laughed. "You think?" he teased. "You're known for being an advocate for change Mom."

Amelia chuckled. "I wasn't much of an advocate for change when I was young," she admitted. "When I was a teenager my grandfather tried to teach me how to talk with my father, who wasn't prone to listening, and I wouldn't give up the fight. He constantly encouraged my father and me to stop yelling and learn to consult, but neither of us was willing to step away from an argument. I did learn about consultation in university, which amused me. I remember he was pleased." She noticed Lucca smile and wondered what he was thinking, he listened so intently. "His name was Michael," she told him, "my brother was named after him."

Lucca was intrigued to hear his mom talk about her life when she was young. He'd never considered what she might have been like, and was surprised to hear she'd been feisty as a teenager. She usually kept herself on a pretty even keel in his observation, and if any word could be attributed to her way of being, it would be diplomatic. "Did Dad know him?" he asked.

Amelia's smile faded and she straightened up, dropping her arm to the table. "No. He passed away when I was away at university, a month before my brother died in a car accident. I met your father later." She rose and took her coffee mug to the sink. "That was a long time ago."

Lucca was struck by how calmly she spoke of their death. "That must have been tough, losing them both like that."

Amelia turned and leaned against the counter, seeing the empathy in her son's face. "It was, but I pretended it wasn't - until I woke up one morning crying and couldn't stop," she confided matter-of-factly. She wanted to minimize the effect of what she said, and wondered how much to share with

Lucca. A little, she decided. "A friend helped me connect with a counsellor, and I met with that man every week for a year. I learned a lot about myself." She turned and opened a cupboard door, taking out a box of cereal as she spoke, purposely completing the conversation with a playful jest. "The moral of the story is 'honesty is the best policy' - especially with yourself."

"Got it Mom," Lucca acknowledged, realizing she couldn't say more. He got up from the table and took his dishes to the sink, smiling as he reached her. He kissed her forehead and moved the conversation on. "I did see Ricco last night," he said, "he filled me in on what you already know, so far so good with the grapes. I'm meeting him at his place." He picked up his hat from the island counter. "Before I go, I also saw Will at the café last night, and he introduced me to a real estate guy who's here talking with him about land in the area. He said he was interested in meeting you, so I told him to drop by. His name's Ned Roberts."

Amelia raised an eyebrow. "Any idea why he wants to meet me?" she asked as if she knew the answer.

"None," Lucca said explicitly. "It has nothing to do with me, honest." He put on his hat, gave her a charming smile and left.

Chapter 3

It was mid-morning before Amelia finished breakfast and got herself going. She headed to the castles, her hat shading her eyes from the bright sun as she strode across the field. The light summer dress she'd chosen offered little protection, and she could feel the burn of the sun on her exposed skin. She saw Emma and Merle as she drew near, tending the vegetable patch that stretched across the backyard of all seven houses. Jack was watching from his porch, and Joe and Sarah were working at the far end of the patch.

Joe and Sarah had come to the valley from a reserve in the north as a young couple. They'd both started working in the orchards for her father when she was in high school, continuing until they retired. They'd always lived in the castles, and raised their children there. Jack had been their neighbor since he came to the valley from the east, working in the orchards for her father for a season, and then taking a job in the vineyards with Alessandro's family. Her father had allowed him to continue to live in the castles, with an agreement that he would maintain them. Jack was skilled and handy, he could fix anything from problem plumbing to a leaky roof. Emma and Merle had moved into the castles three years ago, just after Amelia's mother died. They'd been kids in the foster system most of their lives, and had married at 18 when they aged out of care. They'd both worked in the orchards for a year before taking on the organic vegetable garden project, which Amelia encouraged and supported. Their organic produce was excellent quality and sold well at the local market through the growing season, as well as supplying themselves and everyone in the castles with all they needed. They provided Amelia with produce too, and some of the more prolific plants yielded enough to supply the café.

Amelia reached Nicia's back porch as Nicia pushed open the screen door and came out with a tray of lemonade. She extended it to Amelia and looked toward the friends in the vegetable patch. "They work so hard, even in the heat," she said. "I thought everyone could use a drink."

"Thanks Nicia," Amelia said, appreciating her kindness. She chose a glass and took a long drink. "I was just thinking of how everyone came over the years," she said, looking across the garden, and to Jack. "I can't imagine this not being how it is here."

"Sometimes it's hard to imagine change before it happens."

Amelia turned to her with surprise and Nicia shrugged. "I've heard about Will."

Amelia nodded but didn't comment. "Let me take a drink down to Jack," she offered, picking up a glass and walking the length of the houses to Jack's porch. "Hi Jack," she said, handing him the glass. "How are you feeling today?" She gently placed her hand on the back of his neck. "How about a cool wet cloth back here?" she suggested.

"I'm okay," he wheezed, "don't fuss." He took a drink. "Nicia makes good lemonade," he said, smacking his lips.

Amelia smiled at him. "Yes, she does," she agreed.

"Joe and Sarah," she called to them. "Nicia's brought us lemonade, good time for a break."

They lifted their heads from their work, pushing hats back a bit to see her. Sarah stood and gave Joe a hand to help him up. By the time they reached Amelia, Nicia had walked down to meet them. They took the lemonade with thanks and drank thirstily, removing their hats in the shade of the porch roof.

"How are things at the house Amelia," Sarah asked, "are you able to sleep nights? We're doing fine on the porch, but inside is too hot to sleep."

"Managing so far," Amelia answered. "Are you both feeling well?"

Joe nodded, placing his empty glass on the tray Nicia held. "Just too hot," he said, shaking his loose fitting shirt and long pants free from his body. "Nothing else. We're outside when it cools a little and went to the café yesterday. That was good."

"Yeah," Sarah said, "I think we'll do that every day until this passes. It can't stay so hot forever." She put her glass on Nicia's tray, swept her long loose skirt to one side and sat on the step of the porch.

"Amelia," Joe said with a serious tone, "we heard Will Trumble talking about tearing these houses down and building apartments. Can he do that?"

"No Joe," she answered, "Will's just talking. He doesn't own the land."

"That's a good thing," Sarah stated. "We were wondering where we'd go."

"Let's get more work done while we can," Joe said, turning back to the garden. "Thanks Nicia," he said, patting her shoulder as he walked past.

Sarah stood up, patting Nicia's shoulder too and waving goodbye to Amelia as she followed Joe. "You keep cool Amelia," she called over her shoulder. Small clouds of dust rose around her canvas shoes as she walked through the dry dirt at the edge of the vegetable patch, and disappeared as

E.G. Brook

she stepped onto the moist soil between the rows in the garden.

* * *

Amelia crossed the ball field with a basket of vegetables from Emma, reaching the road as George's dusty truck was pulling into her driveway. He got out of the truck and walked toward her, looking dusty himself in T-shirt and shorts.

"I've got to check the park at the lake," he said. "I thought you might want to come for a swim."

"Yes!" she said with enthusiasm. "Hold on a minute while I get some things." She hurried up the stairs and disappeared into the house.

George sat on a step in the shade while he waited for her. He pulled a kerchief from his pocket and wiped his brow and the back of his neck, adjusting his hat. He stuffed the kerchief back in his pocket as Amelia came out in capris and a shirt, a couple of towels draped over her arm, a cloth bag in hand. George rose and circled around the truck, climbing in the driver's seat as she climbed in through the passenger's door.

"I've got focaccia in here as well as water," she informed him as she placed the bag on the seat between them. "I might get hungry," she teased.

George chuckled. "Ever thoughtful."

The parking lot was empty when they arrived. George grabbed gloves and a garbage bag from the back of the truck and set out checking for litter, his main concern being anything combustible or reflective. Amelia headed toward shade trees that had been planted amid the vegetation bordering the sand decades ago. She dropped her bag and towels in the shade, briefly watching the sun glisten on the surface of the lake before looking further down the shore to the public beach. It seemed people were staying out of the midday heat, there were only three children splashing in the water with their parents. Amelia wondered about the wisdom of being there midday herself, and instantly dispelled the thought. She chuckled to herself, remembering how often her mother had told her swimming and staying in wet clothes would keep her cooler throughout the afternoon.

She took a water bottle from her bag, unscrewed the cap and took a drink before closing it and dropping it on a towel. She ran quickly over the hot sand and into the water, welcoming the silky feeling of it around her legs. George splashed in beside her, shirtless, eager to get wet. She laughed, enjoying how much they both loved the water.

"You coming?" he asked, not waiting for an answer, but diving in and swimming toward a floating dock not far off shore. Amelia willingly slid into the lake, swimming with an ease born of skill developed over a lifetime. She lingered in the cool, deep water a few feet from the dock, watching George pick a spot on the wooden deck and sprawl out contentedly.

His reconnection with her family when he'd returned after so many years initially surprised her, and she remembered how glad her parents had been to see him. She'd thought at the time it was his association with Michael they'd welcomed; he'd brought back some good memories. As she and Alessandro got to know him better she'd realized he was like Michael in several ways; gentle, caring, kind. He and Alessandro had hit it off immediately, and the kids grew to think of him as family. She considered him one her best friends. After Alessandro had passed five years ago, George's friendship supported her adjustment to being on her own, and they'd grown closer. There was a natural boundary to their relationship they both seemed to understand, but over the last year she'd noticed him uneasy with it.

"I remember when Michael and I used to swim here after

working in the orchards," George said, sitting up on the dock. "It still is the best way to cool off."

Amelia swam the few feet to the ladder, grasped it and climbed onto the dock. She lifted her clothes lightly away from her body and sat down next to George, her hair dripping water down her back. Without thinking she reached around and brought her hair forward over her shoulder, gently squeezing water onto the dock as she had countless times. "I remember you two together," she said, taking advantage of him mentioning Michael to say more. "You and Michael were such good friends we hardly ever saw you apart. I'd forgotten you'd worked in the orchards."

"You weren't around much then. We started during your last year of high school and you were always off with some guy."

Amelia laughed. "You noticed that?" she said, surprised.

"Sure," George said. "I had a crush on you."

"George, you were only ten years old!"

"No matter," he said and grinned, but his smile faded. "Is that a problem, that I'm younger?" he asked seriously. "Age difference doesn't matter anymore."

"Not a problem at all, we've been friends for years," she responded.

"What about being more than friends?" he asked, holding her gaze. She was silent for what seemed like a long minute, turning away briefly and then turning back to him.

"I don't know what to say to that," she admitted. It was the first time he'd spoken of what she sensed was causing his uneasiness; he wanted more.

"Think about it," he said quietly. She nodded yes. He stretched out on the dock, closing his eyes. She gazed at him, wondering about what he'd said, and what had prompted him to say it now. He opened his eyes, shading them with his hand and looking intently at her.

"You know I don't think I've ever seen you in a bathing suit," he commented.

She grinned. "The only time I wore one was swimming in pools when I was in university. My mom taught me to swim in light clothes; she did too. Even in the regular heat here it keeps you cooler after the swim."

George smiled and dropped his hand, closing his eyes. Amelia gazed at him, feeling the attraction he had the courage to acknowledge. She deliberately shifted her attention.

"What was it like George," she asked, "travelling and living away so long?"

"Good," he said. "Different."

"A man of many words," she teased.

He chuckled, opened his eyes and shaded them with his hand, looking at her. "Didn't you ever want to live somewhere else?"

"I did live somewhere else," she said. "I was away at university for four years."

"But you came home when you graduated. Why?"

She looked out over the lake. "I didn't think I would when I left," she admitted, "but four years was enough. Here was home." She smiled a little, turning to him. "And I met Alessandro the summer after graduation, which probably influenced my decision to stay."

"No doubt," George chuckled, dropping his hand and closing his eyes again.

"We got married the summer you graduated and left," she said, pausing thoughtfully. "I don't remember seeing you very often when I came home, before you left. What were you up to back then?"

"Trying to stay out of trouble, biding time. Spent a lot of time with Jack."

Amelia nodded, remembering him as a teenager with Jack.

"I remember now," she said. She couldn't remember any girlfriends. She watched him, wondering; he sensed it.

"Say it Amelia," he said.

"Wasn't there someone special you met sometime, while you were away?"

"No one that made me want to stay," he answered honestly.

"Hmm."

"Hmm what?" he questioned, opening his eyes and squinting at her.

"Just hmm," she teased.

He laughed. "Forget about my love life," he said, getting up, looking at her with a curious expression. "You are a mystery to me."

Amelia laughed. "*I'm* a mystery," she said incredulously. Did he honestly not realize how little he shared of himself?

"Come on," he said, offering her his hand. She took it, allowing him to pull her up. He grinned and dove into the lake.

She dove in after him and took her time moving through the water, enjoying every minute. He stood and waded ashore, she picked up her pace. Something behind him caught her attention, and she focused on it. Smoke! With a rush of fear she shouted to George; he didn't hear. She quickly swam the remaining distance and breathlessly waded ashore, pointing to the sky when he turned to her with a towel.

He turned, saw the smoke and without a word ran toward the truck. She was with him by the time he'd backed up, climbed into the cab and searched her bag for her cell phone. Still breathing heavily she pulled the phone out, pressed 911, and waited impatiently for an answer.

"Fire. Creek Road area, near the school and ball field," she stated, listened for confirmation and ended the call. She pressed the number for Ted; he answered. "Ted, where are you right now?" She listened anxiously. "Can you see smoke? Which direction?" She listened. "Go to the water main and turn all sprinklers on," she directed, looking toward the castles as they neared the ball field; the fire was at the end of them. "Ted, I can see the fire. It's by Joe and Sarah's. Send crew ahead to get people out of there and the subdivision."

The fire was blazing through the dry grass at the edge of the orchard when they arrived. Merle and Joe were shovelling dirt onto it from the road, trying to keep it small. Sarah and Emma were dousing it with water from garden hoses. George grabbed a shovel from the back of his truck and ran to help. He tried to snuff out flames with the shovel, before covering the area with dirt. The wail of sirens grew louder as two fire trucks came into sight and turned onto the road, followed by an ambulance and police car. Amelia stood by George's truck and searched for some sight of Jack, Nicia and Hannah. She saw Jack and Hannah with the baby standing far back from the fire in the shade of the school.

She ran to them. "Where's Nicia?" she asked Hannah urgently.

"She was just here," Hannah answered, looking around.

"I'll find her," Amelia told Hannah. "Let anyone know who asks." She looked toward the subdivision, knowing Nicia would be trying to help. She spotted her on the far side of the ball field, steadily walking toward one of the houses. Amelia ran toward her, calling her name as she got closer. Nicia didn't respond, but banged on the door of the house. Amelia caught up to her as she headed toward a second house; grasped her shoulders, laboring to catch her breath. "First responders will get the people to safety Nicia," she assured her, "we can leave it to them."

"You know better than that Amelia Quinn," Nicia said

with reproach. "We can't wait for others to do what needs to be done."

"Then we go together," Amelia insisted, and they continued on to the second house.

George caught up with them by the time they were at the fifth house, his sweat drenched clothing smeared with dirt. He looked relieved. "It's out," he said. "Fire crew and hoses took care of it pretty quickly. They're looking for signs of what started it."

"Did anyone from the castles see how it started?" Amelia asked.

"No. They were working late in the garden, Emma noticed it and called the others. Good they got on it right away, that made the difference."

Nicia was listening attentively. "I saw a car go down the road and turn around just before it started, a silver one."

"Not a car you know then," Amelia stated.

"No, only a few of Ted's crew drive down there sometimes. They usually park at the school."

Amelia looked from Nicia to George with disbelief. "Do they think someone started it?"

George nodded. "Probably not intentionally, but it's human caused."

Amelia stood in awe. "Who could be so careless in these conditions? It could have spread so quickly and burned all of this," she exclaimed with distress, encompassing everything from vineyard and café through orchards and castles to school and subdivision, with one wide sweep of her arm.

Nicia caught her arm and drew Amelia close beside her. "Don't think about what could have happened Amelia, the fire is out," she said decisively. "Let's go and be with the others." She held Amelia's arm linked in hers and walked back toward the castles. George branched off to get Hannah and Jack at the school.

Ted and some of his crew were standing with the others by the fire trucks, and paramedics were checking Joe as Sarah stood by. Merle and Emma were huddled together near the castles, looking much younger than their years. Amelia moved from Nicia's side and went to them.

"Are you two alright?"

Emma looked on the edge of tears, and Merle's eyes couldn't deny the fear he attempted to hide. "We're okay," he said, then glancing into Amelia's eyes admitted, "It was pretty scary." Amelia touched Emma's shoulder compassionately. "It's over," she confirmed. "We're all okay."

"Amelia!" Ted called to her. She turned and walked to where he was standing by the burnt grass with Nick, the Chief of the Fire Department. Nick was second generation Japanese Canadian, just a few years older than Lucca. His manner had a respectful distinction she admired. He straightened up as she approached, and Amelia welcomed his regard more than she ever had.

"Hello Nick, what did you find?" she asked as she reached him.

"We found a cigarette butt," he responded. "It would have had to land at the right angle to ignite the grass and start the fire, which is rare. It's an unlikely cause, though conditions are prime for that kind of incident. We didn't find anything else, no glass or soiled rag that could have sparked it."

"There's no fueled power equipment used this time of year," Amelia said.

Nick nodded. "Ted confirmed that. He says none of his workers smoke, and they keep the grass clear of debris summers, especially now. We'll look into it further," he stated. "That's all I can tell you Mrs. Marin."

"Thanks Nick," she said. He nodded and motioned to his crew to join him as he climbed into the cab of the fire truck.

Amelia turned to Ted. "Thanks for getting here so fast. I'm grateful it didn't take off."

"Joe said he saw a silver car drive down here and stop. A guy got out and was looking around, then drove away," Ted told her.

"Nicia mentioned the car too," she stated. She closed her eyes a moment, inhaling deeply, feeling the strain of the near miss.

"You okay?" Ted asked, concerned.

She opened her eyes and gave him a weak smile. There was no point in mentioning the incident had shaken her to her core. "I'm fine, just hot," she assured him, lightly lifting her shirt away from her body. Ted nodded, and joined his crew waiting at the edge of the orchard. They headed back among the trees.

George walked up behind her and put his hands on her shoulders, feeling her tension. He turned her around and saw how exhausted she was. "Let's go back to the house," he suggested, not waiting for an answer but moving her toward his truck.

"Good idea," she whispered.

* * *

Amelia wearily climbed the stairs to her porch with George, pausing as she reached the top. George moved to his usual place and leaned against the railing, feeling drained. They both turned to the car that pulled into the driveway.

"A silver car," Amelia said coldly as she watched a man step out of it. He was dressed in beige linen pants and a light green shirt that looked crisp and pristine against his dark skin. Amelia briefly thought of how haggard she and George must look, but dismissed concern the moment the man spoke.

"Mrs. Marin," he said, walking to the bottom of the stairs.

"I'm Ned Roberts, a realtor associate of Mr. Trumble's."

"Hello Mr. Roberts," she said evenly, motioning for him to come up the stairs. "My son mentioned you might drop by." Amelia had no idea how she would find the will to be civil to this man, but determined she must.

He climbed the stairs and extended his hand to George, who shook it, then to Amelia, who motioned toward a wicker chair.

"Please sit down," she said. "Would you like something cool to drink?"

"Don't bother yourself," he said.

"No bother," Amelia assured him, and turned to George. "Drink George?"

George nodded yes. Ned sat down, and Amelia went into the house.

"This is a small town Mr. Roberts," George said, feeling obligated to give the guy a heads up. "I imagine you've heard everyone knows everybody here, if you've come into town to do business."

Ned smiled. "I have been told that Mr. -- I'm sorry, I don't know your name."

"George."

"George," he repeated, sitting back in the chair, weighing the situation. "I've also heard it's a friendly town," he added.

"Most times," George said, his expression an unmasked warning it could be otherwise.

Amelia came out of the house carrying a tray with three glasses of iced tea, her face cleaned, hair brushed and loosely tied up off her neck with a scarf. Her clothes were dry after the swim and she looked like she'd gotten her second wind. She held the tray toward Ned and he politely took a glass. George stepped forward and took one, drinking thirstily. Amelia put the tray on the coffee table, taking the last glass for herself.

"Please excuse us Mr. Roberts," she said frankly, "we've just been dealing with a fire." Now he knew what ground they were standing on; fragile, with risk of explosion. She took a long drink, and sat down in the other wicker chair.

Her frankness unnerved Ned momentarily. He clearly recognized the warnings from both George and Amelia that this meeting could be volatile, but had no idea why. "I'm sorry," he said, sitting forward. "Perhaps I should come by another time."

"No need," Amelia said. "I'm curious to know of your purpose here."

Ned regained his sense of advantage, sipped the iced tea and placed the glass on the table, sitting back in his chair. He'd give it his best shot. "Then I'll get right to it," he said. "I work in real estate Mrs. Marin, and Will Trumble has recently been in touch with me asking for my assistance. I understand he has a development project he's looking for land for, and your family owns the piece he's interested in."

"That's right," Amelia confirmed.

"My specialty is negotiation Mrs. Marin, bringing the two parties together if a sale doesn't at first seem profitable," he said. "I've met with Mr. Trumble several times, and belief I can help you two out."

"I'm in no need of help Mr. Roberts," she stated. That second wind was quickly dissipating.

"Well perhaps you'll hear me out?" he asked.

"Go ahead," she agreed.

"When Mr. Trumble first approached me his main concern was gaining access to your relative's contact information in Ontario, a Mr. A. J. Quinn who reputedly owns the land," he informed her and paused, watching for her reaction. She offered him none. He continued, "With a little research I was able to find an obituary notice for a Mrs. A.J. Quinn of Wallaceburg, Ontario, a recently deceased elderly lady, who was pre-deceased by her husband. They had no children."

"You're quite resourceful Mr. Roberts," she said.

"I'm very inquisitive as well Mrs. Marin," he added, "which led to my discovery through conversation with your son, that your maiden name was Quinn, and your given name is Amelia."

"Right again," she stated, "and your point?"

"Could you be the A.J. Quinn designated as the owner of the land in question? In fact, the owner of all the Quinn family land in the area?"

Amelia met his gaze silently, holding it with a searing look. She took another drink of iced tea, wondering where he would go with his premise.

Ned looked at her intently and leaned forward. "Do you object to my being a black real estate agent Mrs. Marin?" There had to be some reason for her icy attitude.

"Why would I?" she questioned calmly.

He didn't respond. She felt as if he was playing cat and mouse.

"Because I'm an old white lady?" Amelia asked wryly, playing back the stereotype. He said nothing, but his expression registered his surprise. She felt a wave of empathy, despite annoyance with his manner. "I imagine you've experienced a lot of difficulties because of your skin color Mr. Roberts, I don't deny that. That bias isn't happening here, so let's set aside the stereotypes," she suggested. He didn't respond.

She turned away, reaching within herself for greater diplomacy, for a way to get them to common ground. She looked over the field toward the castles as she spoke. "Your comment brings something to mind. When my daughter was a little girl, I learned that skin color has to do with where our ancestors lived, and the amount of melanin we have in our bodies," she said matter-of-factly, and turned back to him.

His veiled expression communicated that whatever he was thinking or feeling, it was well hidden beneath a complacent mask. "A very long time ago our ancestors, yours and mine, lived close to the equator," she continued, "and mine moved more and more north, which very gradually over a long period of time led to the evolution of a lighter color of skin." She paused. Ned remained silent. "I find that fascinating. If they'd stayed put, we wouldn't be having this conversation," she concluded.

Amelia rose from her chair and paced a few steps toward the stairs. "In my eyes we're all people Mr. Roberts, part of the same human family. Sometimes we have to work to get along," she stated, turning toward him. "Judging by how this meeting is going, I'd say perhaps this is one of those times."

He abruptly stood up, unimpressed, showing slight irritation beneath his professional demeanor. "There is something you object to."

"Yes!" she said vehemently. "I object to the manner with which you're approaching me." She faced off in front of him. "I don't know your character, and I feel uncertain about your values. Neither encourages me to do business with you." She walked away from him to get hold of her irritation. She turned and sighed, softening her manner. "I prefer to work collaboratively Mr. Roberts," she told him evenly. "I'd appreciate both you and Will Trumble giving that consideration before being in touch with me again."

He brushed by her without a word, quickly descending the stairs.

"Mr. Roberts," she called to him as he reached his car. "You are in the country. Please dispose of cigarette butts and any other burning material carefully."

He looked stunned, quickly got into his car and drove away.

She sighed and shook her shirt loose from where it clung

to her, turned and picked up the tray of glasses from the coffee table. "I need to find Lucca," she said to George over her shoulder, hoping she would get to Lucca before he ran into Ned. "Would you drive me to the café?"

"Sure," George responded. He opened the screen door for her as she headed toward the house. "Melanin?" he asked quizzically as she approached him.

"Julia loved Bill Nye the Science Guy," she explained, and shrugged as she walked by him. George chuckled. She glanced at him and stopped short. He was still filthy from fighting the fire. "George, you're a mess," she blurted.

"Well you have water inside don't you?" he said unphased. She laughed in spite of herself and walked into the house. He smiled and followed her.

Chapter 4

The café was busy when they arrived. Amelia and George scanned the clientele looking for Lucca; he wasn't there. They spotted Emma and Merle looking much happier, seated at a table with Nicia, Phil, Hannah and the baby. Hannah was chatting with Capriana as she handed out menus. Sam, Jack and Ted were eating at another table. George nudged Amelia, motioning toward Ricco and Lucianna seated nearby.

"Amelia, George," Lucianna called, noticing them by the door. "Sit down here you two and have dinner with us."

"Thanks," George said as they reached the table, pulling out a chair for Amelia to sit next to Ricco, which she quickly slid into. He seated himself next to Lucianna.

"How are you two doing?" Lucianna asked. "We heard about the fire."

"Glad it's over," George replied.

"I was hoping to find Lucca here Ricco, do you know where he is?" asked Amelia.

"Will dropped by earlier and they went to the lake," Ricco said. "A good thing for Lucca, he's finding working in this heat pretty hard."

"Here he is," Lucianna said, nodding toward the door. Amelia turned and saw Lucca walking toward them.

"I thought I'd find you here when you weren't home," he

said, moving a chair over from a nearby table and sitting down. "What's great for dinner Lucianna?"

"Everything, and you're just in time to order," Lucianna said with a smile, motioning to Capriana who walked over to the table with menus.

Amelia put her hand on Lucca's shoulder, leaning forward as he turned toward her. "Have you seen Will's realtor this afternoon?" she asked quietly.

Lucca gave her a puzzled look. "No, why?"

Amelia dropped her hand to her lap and sat back in her chair, relieved. "I'll tell you when we get home," she promised.

* * *

It was dusk when George pulled into her driveway to drop them off. "Please come in," Amelia requested when he left the truck idling. "I've something important to tell you and Lucca."

George turned off the truck obligingly, and walked inside with them.

"Take a seat you two," Amelia stated as she crossed the living room and turned on a lamp. She slid the scarf from her hair and set it on the sofa end table as Lucca dropped into the armchair closest to him. George sat in the other, leaned back and closed his eyes.

"George?" Amelia questioned, empathizing with the fatigue but wanting his attention.

He opened his eyes and straightened up, noticing the night was growing darker in the window behind her. Amelia sighed; he realized she was waiting for him.

"Sorry," he said, turning to her. "A little tired."

"Okay," she said, uneasily standing before them by the sofa. "I don't know where to start," she admitted, and glanced from one to the other, settling her attention on

Lucca. "The realtor you mentioned dropped by today Lucca, and considering how that went I need to tell you about ownership of the Quinn orchards."

"I know relatives own the orchards Mom," Lucca said, "can it wait? I told Ricco I'd meet him earlier tomorrow."

"No Lucca, I own them," she corrected. "I've been wondering how to tell you and Julia for years. Now I feel caught in a lie I never made."

Lucca stared at her, stunned. "What are you talking about?"

Amelia paced as she spoke. "You know my father left the land to A.J. Quinn, generally believed to be a cousin of mine living in Ontario. A.J. Quinn refers to me, Amelia Jane Quinn. The belief otherwise is hearsay my father hoped for, and my mother allowed. It's related to how the land became my father's, the second son in his family, when his older brother didn't return here after the Second World War. Instead he settled in Wallaceburg, Ontario, with his young Belgian wife. The family never spoke of him afterward, they let everyone who'd known him as a boy believe he was living happily back east. In truth the war had ravaged him. He'd become an alcoholic, and died in 1959. My grandfather left the land to my father. His eldest son's name was Adam John."

"A.J. Quinn," Lucca acknowledged, stating the obvious.

"Yes," Amelia confirmed, rubbing her sweaty palms over the sides of her capris as she continued to pace. "Of course my father intended to pass the land on to my brother Michael. When Michael died so young, only twelve, my father was devastated. I realized later he didn't deal with Michael's death, in some ways he carried on as if it hadn't happened."

George shifted uncomfortably in his chair, turning away from Amelia.

"My mother and I thought his grief was what kept him from talking about passing the land on," she continued, "and we just let it be."

Amelia stopped pacing and looked earnestly at Lucca. "We had no idea what he'd actually done. It wasn't until he died that we discovered he'd left the land to me, with a request that public title be A.J. Quinn, and only my mother and the lawyers be advised that it referred to me."

Lucca could see the memory was difficult for her. "Mom, you don't need to explain," he said.

"I do," she stated. "He clarified details in a letter to my mother, stating his reason for the secrecy was to protect me from unwanted attention, to negate problems a woman might encounter owning so much land." She paused and sank onto the sofa, looking down at her hands. "People assumed A.J. Quinn was my uncle's son and namesake. My mother didn't deny it."

Lucca leaned back in his chair, quietly assessing his mother's mood. She was hurting. "Amelia Jane Quinn. You own over 100 acres of orchards, and Grandpa didn't want anyone to know. Unbelievable." He kept his eye on her. "I remember when he died, I was fifteen," he stated. "I had no idea any of this was going on."

Amelia felt powerless to explain what had never made sense to her, yet felt she must. "Women were seen with such bias back then Lucca, it's hard to understand if you've never known it - despite the bias that still exists," she emphasized. "He'd drawn up his Will soon after Michael died, when I was nineteen and in university. When he passed, I was a married woman with two children, a university degree, and years of experience working in broadcast news. I was working with Alessandro and keeping the books for the vineyards. None of that mattered, I was his daughter and not his son. It was that basic to him." She saw the confusion in Lucca's face, and realized she'd have to bridge generations to alleviate it. How could she do that? A simple statement about how she'd dealt with her father's attitude was all she could manage. "I gave up trying to change his mind by the time I was thirteen," she confided.

"I'm speechless Mom. I don't know what to say," Lucca admitted.

Amelia sighed. "I can imagine," she said quietly. "His request for secrecy essentially gagged my mother and me, and we choose to honor it."

George sat forward in his chair, unable to be quiet any longer. "And stuff the anger."

Amelia looked at him with surprise. "You remember?"

"Yes," George responded with an intensity unlike him. "Michael knew how you felt about your Dad's attitude. I'd been back here for about a year when your Dad passed, and I remember the day the Will was read. I just didn't know what you were so mad about."

Amelia turned away, her eyes brimming with tears.

"I was with Alessandro and the kids when you and your mother got back from reading the Will," George continued. "You never came into the house, your mother did. She looked at Alessandro without a word. He got up and left; said he was going to walk to the vineyard with you."

Amelia wiped her eyes with the back of her hand. "Alessandro knew me so well," she affirmed, looking up and steadying her voice. "My father didn't. I don't believe he would have left the land to me if he'd had another choice."

"It was a good choice," George said sincerely, "no matter how your father came to it."

"What do you mean?" Amelia asked, confused.

"What you've done," George stated, amazed to realize she couldn't see what was so obvious to everyone else. Amelia continued to look puzzled. "Shall I make a list?" he asked with half a smile. "You made the transition to organic and improved the quality of the fruit; the reputation of the orchards grew and took you to a whole new level of operation. You sponsor local sports teams, and open the orchards to teachers who want to tour with students and learn about organic gardening. You give a bursary to a high school grad every year. You donated land to the town for the subdivision, the school and the ball field to be built," he concluded. "You've made things better Amelia," he emphasized.

Amelia smiled, appreciating his acknowledgement of her efforts. "You're a kind man George," she said warmly.

George threw up his hands in resignation. Lucca chuckled. Amelia turned to Lucca to speak, but hesitated. He noticed and turned his full attention on her. "What Mom?" he asked, feeling hesitant to hear what more she might say.

She shifted forward on the sofa. "Your dad and I had a wonderful relationship Lucca. He helped and supported me in so many ways, including resolving the issues I had with my father. Eventually I was able to let the anger go," she stated. "We made a choice together I've wanted to tell you about for a long time."

Lucca relaxed and smiled. "Please don't tell me you weren't married," he joked.

Amelia smiled. "We definitely married," she said, remaining sincere, "and when we did, I didn't legally take your father's name."

Lucca stared at her in disbelief. "Mom, you've always been called Mrs. Marin. Friends, teachers, everybody."

"And I am Mrs. Marin," Amelia insisted, "but adding his name to mine would have involved legally changing my name on my birth certificate, which we both thought was ridiculous."

Lucca slumped back in his chair. "I don't get it," he

confessed.

"It was the '70s,"Amelia said, imploring his understanding. "I was determined to keep my last name, it meant a lot to me. It was a connection I had with my grandfather. If I took your father's name I would have had to give it up. A woman basically lost her identity when she married, and I didn't want any part of carrying that on." She paused, but Lucca gave her no sign of what he was feeling. "Being called Mrs. Alessandro Marin wasn't going to fly," she stated.

Lucca laughed uncomfortably. "I can see that," he admitted.

Amelia continued with reassurance, "Your father understood, and we made it work for both of us. I was called Mrs. Marin, I referred to myself as Amelia Quinn Marin, and my signature became my version of Amelia. No one ever noticed there was no last name included."

Lucca took a deep breath and laid his head back on the chair. "This is a little weird Mom."

"I know. I'm sorry I couldn't choose a time to tell you and Julia about all this sooner." She sat back with a sigh. "Now Ned Roberts believes I'm the A.J. Quinn who owns the land, and is probably planning to use it to get Will the castle land for his project."

Lucca lifted his head. "Does it matter if people know?" he asked innocently.

"This is a small town, there could be friction about the secrecy. It might change how people think of me," Amelia responded, feeling a vulnerability that worried her. She wiped dampness from her cheeks and lifted her hair back from her face, attempting to move past the feeling. "I honestly don't know how things might change," she admitted.

"This build seems too important to Will to make sense,"

George interjected. "I think there's more to it."

"His Dad's sick," Lucca told them. "I think he needs the project to leverage loans. He wants to get his Dad to the coast for treatment."

Amelia looked at Lucca with concern. "I hadn't heard about Fred being sick."

"Will mentioned it when asking me about accommodation in the city," Lucca stated. He looked away uncomfortably.

Amelia sensed Will had been asking about more than accommodation in the city. "Has Will been asking you about the land Lucca?" she questioned him. He hesitated to answer. "Lucca?" she persisted.

"I think Will has his eye on the Quince Road land too, the piece that wasn't planted."

"The 27 acres next to the apple orchards?" Amelia asked. Lucca nodded yes. "How do you know Will's interested in it?"

"I don't know for sure. He was asking about zoning," Lucca replied.

"It's agricultural," Amelia stated. "It could be subdivided to allow a residence on a smaller acreage, but not into housing lots. I'm planning to keep it available for planting."

"Mom, things are going to change."

"They need to change for good, not greed," she stated emphatically. Lucca shrugged. Amelia apologized. "I'm sorry for snapping Lucca, I'm glad you mentioned it. I'll drive by the acreage tomorrow."

Lucca sighed and stood up. "I'm tired. We need to give this time to sink in. I'm going to bed." He stepped to the sofa and gave Amelia a kiss on the forehead. "I'll see you two tomorrow," he added, giving George a brief nod goodnight as he left the room.

Amelia stood up, relieved it was over. She turned to George. "Thanks for staying and sitting through this George.

It's been a long day, let's say goodnight."

"Stay a minute," George urged, appearing revitalized. "This brought something up for me."

"I'm very tired George."

"Just one question," he assured her.

She sat down again. "One question," she agreed wearily.

He leaned forward earnestly. "Is this why you've held back?" he asked.

Amelia was annoyed. "How can you imagine what I own would have anything to do with how I feel about you?"

George sat back in confusion, desperate for understanding. "What then? Sex?"

Stunned, Amelia looked at him in silence. The feeling soon gave way to amused disbelief. "Sex," she repeated, and chuckled as she stood up. "We are way too tired for this conversation," she stated, dismissing his question and turning toward the door.

George got up and gently caught her arm. "I need to have this conversation," he quietly insisted.

"Okay George," she resolutely stated, turning to him. "Sexuality is not negatively affecting how I feel about you." He waited, his eyes holding her with him. Her manner softened, yielding to his need to understand. "Yes, sex can have a different place in a woman's life when the baby making instinct is gone, but loving desire doesn't disappear." An unguarded tenderness rose within her and she moved closer to him, placing her hand on his chest. "I find you very attractive," she confided. He smiled. She held his gaze. "Though many may not want to admit it, what's most attractive to a woman my age is a warm heart. Perhaps at every age." He wrapped his hand tightly around hers. "There's plenty of sex to be found with men George," she quietly stated. "Love's not so easy to find."

"You know I love you," he assured her, his voice husky

with restrained emotion.

Tears welled up in her eyes. "Yes, in my heart I know you do," she whispered, "and I'm afraid. It's as simple as that." He silently drew her close, comforting her. She rested her head against his chest, her voice insistent. "It hurts too much when you lose someone you love deeply. I don't want to ever feel that pain again."

Tears came to his eyes and he ran his hand over her hair, caressing her. "We are too tired for this conversation."

Amelia gave a weak laugh and lifted her head. "Then kiss me goodnight and go home," she quietly implored.

George smiled and gently lifted her face toward him, kissing her lightly before stepping away. "Sleep well," he said.

He moved to the door and opened it. Amelia smiled, and affectionately caressed his back as he left. She closed the door and briefly leaned her forehead on it, feeling overwhelmed by the emotions that had arisen throughout the evening; that had filled the day. With a sigh, she crossed to the lamp and turned it off, hoping she could sleep. She paused to look out the window behind the sofa. The castles and orchard were silhouetted in moonlight.

* * *

Amelia woke to the sound of birds splashing in the fountain outside her open bedroom window. She'd had the dream again and laid awake for several hours before returning to sleep. Now she woke with resistance, the lack of sleep causing her to feel unprepared and unwilling to encounter the day. She lounged in bed, remembering there had been an English translator in the dream relaying what the elderly man said. Her grandfather had heard him speaking about science and the mind, and lifted her up so she could hear as well. As she reached the height of his shoulders, the crowd had disappeared in a flood of white light that dispersed into rainbow colors, dissolving to reveal the street. Grace had been waiting on the sidewalk. Once again her grandfather had gone to Grace, taken her hand, and said her name. Once again they'd walked away together, and Amelia had been unable to move. She'd been left behind.

Amelia heard her phone ring in the kitchen, and realized she hadn't turned it off the night before. There was no sound of movement, and she imagined Lucca had gone to meet Ricco. With resignation and the willpower that so often sustained her, she threw back the sheet and got out of bed.

The kitchen was still when she entered barefoot in her robe. Lucca had gone as she'd guessed. She moved to the cupboard and took out a glass, pivoted to the island counter and poured herself a drink of water. She drank thirstily, stepped to the fridge and found a note from Lucca held to the door with a basketball magnet. With a chuckle she took it down, wondering where he'd found the magnet.

> *Guessed you wouldn't check your phone so went old school – meet me at the harvest shed in the café vineyard when you can? Maybe around 11? Please text.*

She picked up her phone from the counter, and sent Lucca a text confirming she'd meet him at 11. She checked the number of the call she'd missed, and smiled. George had called.

Chapter 5

Emma carefully stepped between rows in the garden, crouching by a section of green peas to check if pods were ready to pick. A screen door banged shut and she turned toward the castles, pushing her hat back to see more clearly. Strands of her damp, fine hair fell across her eyes as she watched Nicia walk across the porch with a pail of water, and she swept them aside with the back of her hand. Nicia put the pail on the top step of her porch and returned indoors, coming out again with full glasses of water on a tray. Emma stood and walked toward her.

"Come and get something to drink, and get your scarves wet," Nicia called to those working in the garden. "Get yourselves wet," she added with a laugh as Merle scooped water from the pail and splashed his face and arms. He took the scarf from around his neck and dunked it in the water, as did Emma, each taking them out and wrapping them dripping around their necks. Merle took a glass of water and handed one to Emma. Nicia went back into the house while Joe and Sarah walked slowly alongside the garden, untying their scarves. They dunked them in the pail and draped them around their necks, pushing up their sleeves and splashing the remaining water on their arms. They each took a glass of water from the tray and sat on Nicia's steps.

Nicia came from her house with a bowl of water and a sponge. She walked down to where Jack was sitting in the shade on his porch. "Here Jack," she said, putting the bowl on a table next to him and handing him the sponge. "Squeeze water on yourself, you need to keep cool." She took his scarf off, dunked it in the water and wrapped it around his neck again. Jack did as she told him, wheezing with each breath.

Emma came by and put a glass of water on the table for Jack. "Thanks Nicia," she said, and walked to the porch of her own house, picking up two baskets from a table. She headed to the long row of peas.

"Haven't seen Amelia today," Jack said between raspy breaths, dropping the sponge into the bottom of the bowl. "Thought she'd come by." He picked up the glass from the table and took a drink.

"She might be too busy to come today," Nicia said. "I saw Lucca early, before he left with Ricco. He said Amelia was still sleeping, and he'd left a note for her to meet him at the café vineyard."

Jack nodded acknowledgement. "I like it when she comes," he stated, wheezing. "George too."

Nicia smiled and patted his shoulder. "George might drop by the café after work, come with us this afternoon," she encouraged. Jack nodded agreement, coughed, and took another drink of water.

* * *

Amelia drove slowly over the dirt road, yet the dust billowed behind the Mustang convertible, drifting over the acres of vines. She parked roadside behind Ricco's truck and climbed out with her cloth bag in hand. She took a fabric hat from the bag and shook it loose before putting it on, letting it flop over her head. The cotton dress she wore was damp with water that had trickled down from the wet scarf tied around her hair, and felt good in the heat. She shifted the bag up to her shoulder and turned toward the vineyard.

Lucca strode toward her in his loose work clothes, wiping perspiration from his face with his shirt sleeve, a leafy piece of grapevine in his hand. "I thought I'd meet you here and we can walk in to the shed," he said, unconsciously adjusting his straw hat. "I see you're driving Dad's convertible," he teased.

She grinned. "My convertible," she corrected. "It's what I have," she added with a shrug.

He laughed. "As if you don't love it!"

She laughed, walking with him between the rows of vines. "Why am I here Lucca?"

"I thought this would be a good place to talk about Dad's Will. You and Dad did a lot of planning here."

"We did," she said, acknowledging to herself what the vineyard meant to her. She inhaled the fragrance of the grapes, looking over the expanse of vines spread before the sky. It was a place she loved, where calm came to her when she was troubled, where memories brought her happiness. She and Alessandro had worked well together here; at harvest, in crisis, when planning. She remembered how often they'd come to the vineyard to talk things through when life challenges were great, and the day he'd compassionately witnessed her anger about her father's Will. Love rose in her heart as she thought of Alessandro; he was such a good man. She missed him. The familiar ache of sorrow reverberated in her chest. She breathed deeply, allowing it to be. It would pass.

"Lucca, I'm going to have a hard time with this," she admitted.

"You don't know what I'm going to say," he informed her. He stopped and sat on the ground in the shade of the harvest shed, taking a crate leaning against the shed and flipping it over for Amelia to sit on. She sat down and pulled a water flask from her bag, giving it to Lucca. She took another flask for herself and unscrewed the cap, taking a drink.

"You know I'm thinking the worst," she said. "I wish I wasn't." She looked to Lucca for relief.

"Just stop forecasting," he said and smiled, taking a drink of water.

He was so like Alessandro in ways other than his looks, and he didn't realize it. She recognized the diversity between them as well, Lucca's soul expressed itself in interests Alessandro had never had. She wondered if things between them would have been better if Alessandro had been more open to Lucca's ideas. No way to know now, she concluded. Alessandro had chosen to keep the traditional ways in the vineyard, Lucca had chosen to become an engineer.

"I've been asking myself what I would need to be happy taking over the vineyards, and last night an answer came to me," he stated, looking down at the vine he held and rolling it across his fingers. "Opportunity," he said. "When I was growing up, I lived with the limitations you and Dad seemed to be unaware of creating, and it became how I thought it had to be living here. Dad was committed to the traditional ways in the vineyard, proud to carry on the practices of his father and grandfather. He wasn't harsh about it, but he rejected ideas I had without considering them. He had no interest in technologies that were being developed and wouldn't read articles I brought to him." He looked up at her and dropped the vine on the ground. "After hearing how it was between you and Grandpa, I know you understand what that feels like. It wasn't as bad for me, but it was hard. Being his son didn't matter Mom."

Amelia could see his sorrow and feel it reflecting in her. "Come on, let's walk," she said. She stood up and shifted her bag to her shoulder, motioning for him to follow her. Lucca got up and they walked along a row of vines as they talked. "I realized you and your Dad butted heads sometimes," she acknowledged, "but I didn't realize the affect it was having on you. I'm sorry I missed that Lucca."

"It wasn't yours to change," he said. "It was Dad's."

"How did you feel I limited you?"

Lucca stopped and turned to her with a wry smile. "Do you remember how long it took you to allow me to get a driver's licence?"

"Ah," she said, stopping and looking out over the vineyard. "I do."

"You were very overprotective Mom, and I understand why as an adult, losing your brother in a car accident, but as a kid I just wanted to be able to do things."

She breathed deeply, looking down at the ground. "Even now I don't know how I could do that differently with the feelings I have," she admitted. She lifted her face to look at him, regret clearly visible. "It wasn't fair to do that, I'm sorry."

Lucca smiled. "Well we're here now," he said quietly. "We move on."

She smiled at him. "You have a generous spirit Lucca," she stated with affection.

He smiled and took a drink of water. She strode on a few steps, stopping and turning back to him.

"What opportunity do you see for yourself with the vineyards?" she asked.

"Managing when you're ready to pass over the reins, working with Ricco," he said, catching up to her. "I think his family are wanting to carry on after him, and Ricco wants to try new methods and evaluate their success. He's mentioned looking into scanning devices and irrigation sensors. I'd want to keep a crew of workers involved as long as there are people interested in the work," he said enthusiastically. "And

E.G. Brook

I'm thinking of establishing a winery."

"A winery!" Amelia exclaimed. "That's something your Dad and I talked about but never felt ready to do." She smiled at him. "I'm pleased," she said. "What about Julia?"

He gazed over the vineyard. "We need to get her here too. She was pretty clear about wanting to step away from the vineyards, but maybe she'd be interested in a financial partnership if nothing more."

"Okay, let's ask Julia to come," she agreed happily. "This couldn't be better," she declared, pausing for a moment and looking at him thoughtfully. "Unless you said you'd be moving back."

Lucca laughed. "One step at a time Mom. I'll talk with Julia about the changes."

"Leave the news of land ownership to me," Amelia advised. "I need to be the one to tell her."

"Right," Lucca acknowledged, stopping by the roadside. "I'm heading to the café for lunch. Are you still planning to stop by the Quince Road acreage?"

"I'm going there now," Amelia said. "Will you be home by dinner?"

"Maybe sooner," Lucca responded. "This heat's wearing me out more than I expected."

"We're all discovering that," Amelia acknowledged.

* * *

Amelia wondered about Will's interest in the Quince Road land as she drove toward it. She had three apple orchards on Quince Road, in addition to the 27 acres her father had bought when it became available, but illness had prevented him from planting. Alessandro had talked of planting wine grapes there after her father passed and the land came to her, yet they soon realized managing the 150 acres they had in production was more than enough. She'd had it in the back of her mind to plant table grapes someday, but that day hadn't yet come.

She recognized Ned Roberts' silver car parked roadside at the edge of her land, and pulled up behind it. Will and Ned were standing with their backs to the road about a hundred yards in, looking at a large document held between them. A survey map she guessed as she climbed out of her car and walked toward them, speaking only as she reached them.

"Can I help you gentlemen?" she asked evenly.

They started, and turned around. "Mrs. Marin," Will said with surprise, looking like a kid caught in the act of doing something wrong. He had no more words to offer.

Ned was more composed, rolling the paper up as he stepped toward her. "You can help us Mrs. Marin," he said smoothly. "We've been looking over a survey document of this piece of land and are interested in purchasing it."

"The land's not for sale," she said simply.

"It's vacant land," Ned stated, "I'm sure there could be a price that would alleviate your attachment to it."

Amelia smiled wryly at his cocky assurance. "The land's priceless," she stated determinedly. "Its value to me is in food production."

Will stepped up. "Mrs. Marin, if you would hear what I have in mind maybe you'd see it another way," he implored.

Amelia felt empathy for Will in the situation he was in, and focused on his sincerity. "Lucca's mentioned your assistance to your parents Will," she said. "I'm listening."

"I can see how we could build an extensive subdivision of high end housing here, with features maximizing the view of the valley and the lake. It would attract new money to the area. The increase in population would increase the demand for services in the town core, which would increase profits for existing business and attract new ones. Town infrastructure could be developed, and town growth in turn

E.G. Brook

would attract more people to the area."

"Who would benefit from more people being attracted to the area?" she asked.

"Businesses right across the board, and town revenue through taxes," he answered.

"And the rest of us, how would we benefit from such growth?" she questioned. Will was silent. "What I hear suggests increase in population, traffic, noise and stresses on the land and local resources," she continued. "The land and local resources sustain established agricultural production in this valley, and the benefits of that production are far reaching."

"Change is going to happen Mrs. Marin," Ned interjected. "People are already attracted to this valley. Retirees from other provinces and young families from the coast are looking for a little space and more affordable prices. With increased acceptance of employees working remotely from home, younger people have more flexibility with where they live. The climate here is a favorable factor for many."

"The changing climate here is an important factor for all of us to consider," Amelia stated with exasperation. "And it goes beyond the ideals of pleasure, warmth and sunshine. Standing here in this heat is testimony to that," she emphasized. "It's anything but pleasant."

Ned looked to Will and shrugged.

"Mrs. Marin, would you consider a detailed proposal if I presented one to you?" Will asked with persistence.

Amelia stood silently, thinking of her conversations with Lucca, looking out over the valley to the lake in the distance. The view was spectacular. In the last few days Lucca and Ned had spoken the inevitable truth - change was going to happen. Change was happening. Her viewpoint shifted, and she felt an emerging willingness to consider a change of use for the acreage. She could be open to Will's idea and proactively contribute to how the change happened. With determination she turned to Will. "What you propose would affect the whole town and surrounding community Will, it's not simply a matter between us. If it's to be considered, it must be open for consideration by everyone. It would need to go before the community for feedback."

Will stared at her, speechless.

"Are you interested?" she asked.

"I can't see how - " Will began, and Amelia held up her hand to stop him.

"Are you interested?" she repeated.

Will looked to Ned, who held up both hands, bowing out. Will looked down at the ground and paced several steps, then turned to Amelia decisively. "I'm interested," he stated.

"Alright," she said frankly, "we'll need to meet with the town Council and request their collaboration. I suggest you get your proposal ready." She turned to leave and stopped after a few steps, turning back. "Shall we leave together gentlemen?" she suggested.

Will and Ned obligingly walked toward their car; Amelia walked with them.

* * *

Lucca arrived home mid-afternoon. After showering he volunteered to make his favorite pizza from scratch, reminiscent of his teenage years and the recipe he'd mastered with his Nonna Marin. Amelia reminded him of how he'd wanted to change his last name back to the original *Marino* around that time, defying the administrative drop of the "*o*" the family had accepted when they arrived in North America. Lucca felt the old passion, and launched into commentary on the personal sacrifices many immigrants had been forced to make, accepting unsolicited name changes. Amelia hadn't realized he still felt upset about the occurrence in his family's history. She acknowledged his points, adding the good news came with realizing those practices had improved. Lucca shrugged, unappeased. She brought him back to the heritage of the vineyards, and listened as he shared ideas he had for a winery. The pizza was as delicious as she remembered it to be, and they decided to leave clean-up for later and move out onto the porch in the cooling evening air.

Amelia pushed the screen door open with her back and pivoted through the doorway with three full glasses on a tray. She placed the tray on the coffee table in front of Lucca, and handed him a glass. He took it and sipped, comfortably sitting back in the wicker chair.

"You're the only person I know who makes fresh lemonade without sugar," he noted, "and it tastes good."

"Mmm," she murmured, sitting in the other chair and taking a glass for herself. "More refreshing I find. The key is using the right amount of lemon juice."

"How much is that?"

"Less," she said with a smile.

"Who's the third glass for?" Lucca asked.

"George," she replied. "He usually drops by."

Lucca looked at her curiously for a moment. She noticed, and met his gaze.

"What's going on with you two?" he asked.

"Good question," she responded casually.

"That's non-committal," he said.

Amelia chuckled. "Presently it is non-committal," she agreed.

They heard George's truck pull into the driveway, the cab door shut, and his footsteps on the stairs.

"Hi George," Lucca called.

"Hi," he said as he reached the top of the stairs, picked up the glass of lemonade, and leaned against the porch railing as he usually did. He took a long drink and looked at Amelia, who was smiling. He turned to Lucca, also smiling. "What are you two up to?" he asked dubiously.

"Same as you," Amelia said. "Trying to keep cool."

"Mmm," he acknowledged, taking another drink. "I heard you're doing much more than that Amelia," he stated.

She laughed. Lucca looked surprised.

"How did you hear anything in just a few hours?" he asked.

"Small town offices," George said. "Will stopped by late this afternoon to see Steve." He looked to Amelia. "Word's out that you're the A.J. Quinn who owns the land. Reaction so far is surprise."

Amelia sat back in her chair, subdued. "Okay," she acknowledged, and took a drink of lemonade.

"Who's Steve?" asked Lucca.

"Planning and Development," George explained. "Were you in on this with her?" he asked Lucca.

"Not directly," Lucca answered, "but I bet she can pull it off."

"No doubt," George agreed, and finished his glass of lemonade. "She owns the land," he stated.

"That's not what this is about," Amelia protested.

"I know," he said, putting his glass on the tray and moving over to sit on the porch swing. "And I also know you're going to play that card," he added.

"You don't think this can work," she challenged him.

"I don't see how," he said with a matter-of-fact tone. "Sure we're a small town and surrounding community," he noted. "*Of about 3,000 people,*" he emphasized as he leaned forward. "Honestly Amelia, how can you imagine getting that many people to agree on anything, one way or the other?"

"The intention is to provide opportunity for people to know about what's being proposed, and to say what they

E.G. Brook

have to say about it," she explained. "Constructively," she added, "not destructively."

"Then what?" George asked.

"What input comes through community will be the basis of consideration when deciding what can be done," she stated.

"Who decides?" he persisted.

Amelia finished her lemonade and put the empty glass on the tray. "The three collaborating parties. Final consultation will happen between the town Council, Will, and myself, with the goal being to reach agreement on a decision."

George looked at her gravely. "Are you telling me you'll allow the castles to be torn down if that's decided?"

"That can't be decided without providing for the people who live there George, that's part of the whole discussion. Will's putting two proposals forward, one involves the castles, the other the 27 acres we've never planted. I'm interested in hearing what people have to say."

George spoke earnestly, "Why are you doing this?"

"Because I can," Amelia answered honestly. "I'm in a position to, and willing to take the risk. It's time." She paused a moment, making an effort to calm her rising passion. "Twice it's been brought to my attention that change is inevitable, and I realized I'm already living it." Her effort to remain calm was unsuccessful; her energy was rising. "This heat wave is more extreme and it's lasting longer. Will it be enough to warrant action on the world stage, this and all the other extreme weather events happening around the world?" she questioned, her voice growing louder. "Will I lose my crops this year? Next year? I don't know the answers."

She stood abruptly and moved to the porch railing, firmly grabbing hold and looking to the castles in the distance. "When Will asked if I'd consider a proposal for the Quince

Road property I decided I would, if he would put it before the community." She turned to George with passionate conviction. "Change is inevitable, okay. Let's be proactive in determining what change occurs when we can have some influence, because there are going to be changes we can't do anything about." She turned away from him and paced along the top of the stairs as she continued. "I can't see where this is going. It's like choosing a path at dawn, you give it your best shot and hope you end up where you want to be." She stopped, turning to face George directly. "I want to be living life on another path, not the one I witness leads to ignoring the most important issues, including being able to afford a home. If Will wants a development project to go ahead, let him hear from the community, consider who benefits, who doesn't, and weigh the balance."

George said nothing.

Lucca broke the silence. "The ball's rolling George," he said. "We've got to see how it plays out."

George shrugged in resignation.

"What's the alternative?" Amelia demanded. "The usual path of pushing through a development with a narrow vision of profit and gain for a few, then we all live with the unhappiness, criticism and fallout of those adversely affected by it?" She looked at him angrily. "How do you see that being a better choice George? Because it's the one we're all familiar with?"

She didn't wait for his response, but crossed to the coffee table and picked up the tray of glasses. She stood for a moment and closed her eyes, reining in her anger before turning to George once more. "Have a little faith," she said with an element of calm. "Not all the powers that be measure in dollars and cents." She headed inside.

"I'm going to pretend I know what she means by that," said George.

"I think we both know what she means," Lucca stated with a slight smile.

George sighed, taking off his hat and putting it on the swing beside him. He pulled a kerchief out of his pocket, wiping his face and the back of his neck before putting it back. He briefly massaged his head, ruffling and smoothing his hair. "I wish those powers that be would ease up on the heat," he said, rubbing his fingers in small circles on his temples. "I'm beginning to feel my age."

"The forecast is for a cooler front to come in tomorrow, with temperatures dropping closer to seasonal for the next week," Lucca told him. "Still hot, but liveable."

"Liveable would be good," George stated. He looked toward the door to the house. "What's she doing in there?"

"Probably getting dessert," Lucca answered with a grin. "She needs to do something when she gets mad."

"Good to know," George acknowledged. He heard her coming to the screen door and got up and held it open for her.

"Thanks," she said, noticeably calmer. She put the tray on the table and handed Lucca a plate with cheesecake and a fork. "Did Lucca tell you Julia's coming?" she asked George as she handed him dessert. She took the final piece and returned to the wicker chair.

"No, he didn't mention it," George commented casually, sitting on the porch swing. "Is she coming soon?"

Lucca nodded. "We had a marathon call with her late this afternoon. I told her about some new thoughts I have for the vineyards, and Mom talked with her about owning the orchards. It was a bit much for one call, but she handled it."

"She might be here by the weekend if David can come as well, or tomorrow if she's travelling on her own," Amelia added. "Lucca can you pick her up at the airport if she comes tomorrow? I'm in the orchards with Ted all afternoon."

"Sure," he answered. "That will give me the hour drive home to hear anything new she's got to say about inheriting the vineyards."

"Late tomorrow morning Will and I are meeting with the Mayor," Amelia said to George. "I'm hoping a scheduled meeting with the town Council will come out of that."

George smiled, commenting with conscious encouragement, "Good. I hope it goes well." Amelia dubiously raised an eyebrow. "Honestly," he added, "here's to no conflict." He grinned, and with a flourish lifted a forkful of cheesecake as a toast and ate it enthusiastically. Amelia chuckled.

Chapter 6

Moonlight filtered through the sheer curtains hanging motionless over the open window as Amelia crossed to her bed, gently lifting the cotton nightgown away from where it clung to her. 'Sweet dreams' George had said as he left, which would be a contrast to the day, she mused, sliding under the sheet on her bed, surrendering to the waves of fatigue rippling through her as she laid down. Dreams could be unbound and revealing, there was a certain sweetness in that. She closed her eyes, hair clinging to her brow, her face damp with perspiration. The soft whirring of the ceiling fan lulled her to sleep, fleeting images dissolving as consciousness released her to the closeness of a crowded room and the warmth of an indistinct male voice.

She was smaller than the suited men surrounding her, hats in hand, and the women in long dresses wearing elaborate hats. Amelia stood out in stark contrast in her childhood play clothes, yet nobody seemed to notice. A young man next to her reached down and took her hand, leading her toward a door. She looked up, happily recognizing her grandfather Michael, willingly following him out into the bright sunlight. He stopped on the walkway, putting his hat on, looking toward a little dark-haired girl in a simple dress she saw watching them from a distance. He turned his eyes to Amelia and smiled.

"What did the man translating into English say as we were leaving?" she asked him.

"He said the elderly man was speaking about science and the mind, about people being able to discover how things really are," he answered.

"No," she protested, "what did he actually say? There were words I've never heard before."

He crouched down in front of her, looking directly into her eyes as he spoke. His image dissolved into the words he said written on a page in a book.

"On the other hand," the words appeared before her, "it is evident and true, though most astounding, that in man there is this supernatural force or faculty which discovers the realities of things and which possesses the power of idealization or intellection. It is capable of discovering scientific laws, and science we know is not a tangible reality. Science exists in the mind of man as an ideal reality. The mind itself, reason itself, is an ideal reality and not tangible."

The image of her grandfather reappeared and he touched her cheek gently, stood up and looked over her head. He walked past her and as Amelia turned around, shading her eyes with her hand in the bright sunlight, she saw him approach the little dark-haired girl. He smiled as he reached her, taking her hand. He affectionately said her name, Grace, and the little girl smiled up at him. They turned together and walked away from her. Amelia tried to call out, but she couldn't. Sadness rose inside her and she tried again to call out, distressed. The little girl stopped and turned toward her. She looked directly at her and smiled.

Startled, Amelia dropped her hand to her side. Her grandfather and the little girl disappeared in the bright sunlight. She turned back toward the sandstone building

E.G. Brook

she'd left, but there were no longer people from the crowd lingering there. A black man in contemporary clothing stood in front of an open doorway, an Asian woman in dress pants and a blouse sat at a table in front of a laptop computer.

A young dark-haired woman in a simple dress and blazer walked toward the table, two men protectively walking on either side of her. The man in the doorway recognized her and smiled. "Grace," he said with friendly regard. "How wonderful to see you've safely arrived. There was concern your travel wouldn't be possible."

"There were threats before our departure, no incidents," Grace told him as she lifted her arm and extended her hand toward him, a thin grey bracelet on her wrist. He reached out and took her hand, a black band on his wrist emitting a green light as it neared her bracelet. He nodded approval and stepped to one side of the doorway. She smiled, lowering her arm.

The woman seated at the table entered data in the computer. "Several members have faced difficulties with travel unfortunately. We're not sure how many will be present for the meeting," she mentioned, looking up at Grace. "The late change to this location doesn't seem to have dealt with interference as was hoped. Acceptance of the authority of the Tribunal continues to be resisted, despite the years of transition."

The man by the doorway looked at Grace with resignation. "It's a slow climb to accountability and collaboration," he said. "It's hard to imagine sustainable peace in the world."

Grace touched his shoulder encouragingly. "Often more than we imagine is possible," she assured him. She nodded to the men with her. One man walked through the open doorway before her and she followed him, the second man close behind her.

The image of the building began to fade, the man and

woman dissolving into the light of a clear blue sky. Amelia
could hear the sound of birds in the distance, of moving
water. She recognized the sound of waves, the cry of gulls
growing louder. In an instant a vast ocean lay before her,
waves rippling across its surface in a warm wind.

Amelia woke with a start, her eyes drawn to the movement
of the sheer curtains over her bedroom window. In the breath
of a warm wind they lifted and swirled in the moonlight, no
longer veiling the window with stillness. The dream played
over and over in her mind; hours passed before she returned
to sleep.

She felt disoriented when she woke in the morning, and
doubtful about having had enough sleep to be her best at the
meeting with the Mayor. It was 9:45 when she walked into
the kitchen completely dressed and ready to leave. Her
meeting was at 10:30. She poured herself a glass of water
and drank as she read a note left on the island counter. Lucca
was meeting Julia at the airport at 4pm and wanted the three
of them to have dinner at the café; he'd pick her up when
they dropped off Julia's suitcase. She grabbed a muffin from
the basket on the counter and headed out the door to walk to
the Municipal Centre, hoping that would clear her head.

* * *

The Mayor's office was the only one in the building that
offered any privacy, being at the end of the hall past the
Council meeting room. George waited for Will and Amelia to
come out, occasionally glancing down the hall at the closed
door. Finally it opened, and the three of them walked out.
Will looked distracted, something else was on his mind. The
Mayor seemed preoccupied as well. Amelia looked toward
him and indicated she wanted to talk with him, then said
goodbye to the two men and walked quickly to his doorway.

"George, could you give me a ride home?" she asked

hurriedly. "The meeting ran late and Ted's picking me up to tour the orchards in about 15 minutes. I walked over, but don't have time to walk home."

"Sure," he said, getting up from his chair and grabbing his hat from a shelf.

Amelia gave him a bullet report as they walked down the hallway. "We'll be meeting with the Council. Step one accomplished," she said.

"Glad to hear it," George acknowledged, admiring her determination. He pushed the Centre door open for her to pass through.

* * *

Ted pulled into Amelia's driveway right after she and George arrived. George got out of the truck to talk with him while Amelia went into the house. She dropped papers on the island counter and disappeared down the hallway for several minutes, coming back with a small backpack. Quickly filling water flasks from the pitcher on the counter, she put them inside the backpack and made herself a protein smoothie with water and a powder mix. She picked up her straw sunhat from the counter and put it on her head, tightened the lid on the smoothie container and shook it as she grabbed her backpack and headed outside.

She stopped to drink by Ted's truck, while he and George finished talking. George looked grim. She decided not to investigate. "Ready to go Ted," she stated and climbed into his truck, noticing he was looking grim as well. "Thanks George," she called to him through the open window. "I'll be at the café with Lucca and Julia for dinner, being brought into the loop of their conversations about the vineyards I hope. I'm going to the castles early tomorrow to see how everyone is, maybe see you then?"

"Give me a call after you're finished with Ted, okay?"

George asked, walking to his truck. She nodded yes, and waved goodbye as Ted backed out the driveway.

"He may want to talk with you about Jack," he said as they drove. "He's not doing well. I was telling him while you were in the house."

"Tell me what's happening," Amelia said with concern.

"Nicia thinks he ought to be in the hospital. She's probably the best one to give you details."

"Let's stop by there now," Amelia suggested.

"Everyone's at the café," Ted said, "which is the best place for Jack to be. Even though it's cooler today, it's too hot for him. If okay with you, I'd like to carry on to the orchards. We've got a lot to do this afternoon."

She nodded agreement. "Okay. What are we looking at with the cherry crop? Has the change in irrigation made a difference?"

"Some," Ted acknowledged, "but I think we got started with it too late. We've lost about 40%."

Amelia looked out the window with dismay, echoing the percentage lost as she watched the truck travel over the passing road. Ted pulled over and parked roadside by one of the cherry orchards. She climbed out and slung the backpack on, following him into the orchard. There were baskets of damaged fruit at the base of every tree.

Ted showed her the condition of the cherries on the lower sections of trees that he considered marketable. "They're not the best we've had," he said, holding a handful out to her. "What do you think?"

"They're small," Amelia said, cupping her hands to receive the cherries. "I'm surprised. I thought the irrigation would have given the trees more, but it looks like it only minimized damage." She rolled the cherries gently in her hand, sniffed them, and put them in her mouth one at a time as they walked. "Taste is okay in some, sweet, juicy. Some taste a bit flat."

Ted wiped perspiration from his forehead with the back of his sleeve. "Give me more than flat Amelia."

She searched for words. "Edgy. Not quite tart, but less sweet; more dry and fleshy." She looked at him as she continued. "As you said, they're not our best, but only a couple were unmarketable in the handful. Care as they're picked will be needed to sort out any too dry. Do you have crews lined up to pick?"

Ted nodded yes. "We're starting early tomorrow morning."

She looked over the orchard, shielding her eyes in the sun. "What a year," she sighed. She dropped her hand and turned to Ted. "Let's carry on."

They returned to his truck and drove on. Amelia spent the next three and a half hours with Ted touring the other cherry orchards, the peach and apricot orchards, and finally the apple orchards. They assessed damage, evaluated maturity, and checked the health of the trees. Ted was well aware of conditions she needed to see, which made good use of their time. As the afternoon drew on, the effects of skipping meals were catching up with her. Despite the seasonal temperatures and attention to keeping hydrated, Amelia felt exhausted by the time they were finished with the apple orchards.

Ted turned his truck into her driveway and stopped, letting it idle as she climbed out. She thanked him and wearily climbed the stairs to the porch. Once inside the house she headed down the hallway to clean up and change before getting something to snack on to get her to dinner. She checked the clock in her bedroom and saw it was after 5, Lucca and Julia would be arriving soon. It was 5:30 when she walked into the kitchen, dropped her bag on the island and opened the fridge, looking for what she could eat. She took a small container of yogurt from the shelf, a spoon from the drawer, and sat down at the island counter. Half way through the yogurt she remembered George. She got up and walked around to her bag, pulled out her phone and called George's number. He answered as she heard Lucca driving into the yard.

"Hi George," she said. "Ted mentioned Jack. How are you doing?" She listened. "Mmm," she murmured, crossing to the window and gazing out toward the castles. "Okay," she acknowledged, listening intently. "He wants to be home, I understand."

Lucca and Julia walked into the kitchen and she held up her hand to let them know she needed a minute. Julia's brown hair was hanging loose over her summer dress, and she dropped a light sweater on a chair as she went down the hall with her suitcase. Lucca sat down at the table. "Lucianna's taking him home after dinner then, and keeping an eye on him. Can you meet me tomorrow morning, and we can talk more with Nicia and the others?" She listened. "Okay, good. Call me anytime, I have the phone with me and it will be on all night." She paced back toward the island counter as she listened. "Good. 'Bye," she said, and ended the call.

She looked at Lucca. "Jack's not doing well," she told him, "and George isn't doing well with the news."

"How not well is Jack?" Lucca asked with concern.

"I don't know," Amelia answered honestly.

Julia walked up behind her and gave her a hug. Amelia turned around and greeted her blue eyed daughter with a wide smile. "Good to see you baby," she said, hugging her.

Lucca laughed. "She said you'd say that," he teased Amelia. "Always the baby," he acknowledged to Julia.

"I can live with it," Julia affirmed, smiling. "The flight was delayed," she added. "We're starving."

Amelia grabbed her bag from the counter. "Okay let's go,"

she said, and turned to Lucca. "Drive please," she requested. He nodded yes, and they headed outside.

* * *

They arrived at the café as Lucianna, Nicia and Jack were leaving. Lucianna gave them a fretful smile, one arm linked in Jack's as he slowly walked toward the door.

"Welcome home Julia. Sorry I can't stop to talk, but we need to get Jack comfortable," she said.

Julia leaned in and gave Lucianna a quick hug, gently touching Jack's arm as he passed. "We'll catch up before I go," she promised.

Lucca silently held the door open for Lucianna. Nicia gave Amelia a knowing look as Jack shuffled through.

Amelia felt a wave of sorrow, and stepped closer to Jack. "Rest easy tonight Jack," she said, lovingly caressing his back. Jack turned and gave her a faint smile. "Let me know if I can help," she said to Nicia, "no matter what time." Nicia nodded.

Lucca led them to a table in front of the windows. Julia seated herself, gazing over the magnificent view of the vineyard in the diffusing light of the early evening sky.

"I'd forgotten how beautiful it is here," she said. "It's such a different beauty than the foothills of Alberta."

"Let's order now and look later," Lucca commented hungrily, signalling Aria.

"Order me a chicken dish," Amelia said, noticing Joe and Sarah across the room. Lucca gave her a questioning look. "Surprise me," she added, and crossed the room to where they were sitting.

Joe saw her coming. "Hi Amelia," he said, and motioned to an empty chair.

"We saw you three come in," Sarah said warmly. "We've visited with Lucca here at the café several times since he arrived. I hope we'll have time with Julia while she's here."

"I'll make sure you do," Amelia assured them as she sat down. "I saw Jack leaving, and Ted mentioned he's not doing well. Can you tell me what's been happening?"

"More difficulty breathing," Sarah said. "It was hard to get him from his house today to come here."

"I went in to check on him this morning when he didn't come out," Joe said. "He usually watches us in the garden for a while. He was still in bed, not sleeping but too weak to get up."

Sarah noticed the emotional pain come into Amelia's face, and reached out to cover her hand with her own. "It's his time soon Amelia, we do our best to keep him comfortable now."

Amelia clasped Sarah's hand gratefully. "Thank you, both of you," she said. "I'm not ready to talk of Jack passing, this is too sudden." Joe and Sarah nodded with understanding. "George and I will come by to see everyone tomorrow morning," she told them, rising from her chair.

"Rest easy tonight Amelia," Sarah encouraged.

Tears welled up in Amelia's eyes with Sarah's uncanny use of the same words she'd just spoken to Jack. She wiped them away with her fingertips as she wove her way back among the tables, and slid into the chair between Lucca and Julia. She sat back for a moment, breathing deeply, willing herself to relax.

"You okay Mom?" Julia asked.

"Yes, just a busy day," Amelia answered, with the measure of truth she was willing to share.

Aria arrived with their order and set the plates before them. Amelia looked at the meal before her as welcome distraction. "This looks amazing," she said thankfully. "I'm so hungry."

She was too tired, too hungry, and too emotional to talk

while she ate, which seemed to work well for both Lucca and Julia. It wasn't until they'd all finished eating and sat with coffee that Lucca opened the conversation.

"Julia and I agree on the plan for the vineyards I mentioned to you yesterday," he said. "Julia's decided she'd like to be partners in ownership when the time comes, and have a consultative role in decision making."

"At the moment I'm feeling kind of excited about it," Julia added, "and I want to spend time in the vineyards while I'm here to test that out." She smiled at Amelia. "We know how I can get excited just because something's new."

Amelia smiled, acknowledging how true that was, and happy Julia recognized it. Julia glanced at Lucca and then to Amelia.

"We're wondering about the orchards Mom," Julia said. "You must have had some thoughts about what you want to do with them."

"A few randomly over the years," Amelia commented, "but nothing concrete."

"What are they?" Julia persisted.

Amelia looked at her daughter thoughtfully. "There's a lot associated with the land and the orchards," she said. "Heritage, a sense of responsibility to those who came before me and worked so hard," she stated. "Now changing markets, and changing climate. I've lost a significant percentage of the cherry crop this year, a little less with peaches and apricots, but still loss. The rest of the growing season is an unknown, and it's hard to forecast how crops will do if hotter summers become the norm."

"Have you thought of selling any of the orchards?" Lucca asked.

"Once or twice," Amelia admitted, "but it never sticks. I can't imagine doing that after all the years the family's owned the land."

"What are the alternatives?" Lucca questioned, prodding her to think more deeply.

"I don't know," Amelia confided. "It was simpler when the land was passed on to the next generation, but neither of you chose an agricultural lifestyle. You're both doing well in your careers, I can't imagine you wanting to take over the orchards."

"I can," Julia stated eagerly. Amelia looked at her with surprise. "I loved being in the orchards with you when I was growing up," Julia continued, "but I always thought they were owned by a cousin in Ontario. I expected he would come and sell them off someday."

"How did I not know this?" Amelia asked with amazement.

"I was surprised too," said Lucca.

Julia shrugged. "It didn't seem worth talking about."

"Julia, honey I'm sorry." Amelia reached out and touched her arm. "I wish I'd known."

"There's nothing to be sorry about Mom, we just didn't know the orchards belonged to you."

Amelia was unprepared for the overwhelming feeling of anguish that flooded her. "How could I let this happen?" she reproached herself. "I had us living a lie all these years." Tears welled up in her eyes, spilling onto her cheeks.

"Don't go there Mom," Lucca ardently intervened. "Grandpa set it up, not you."

She turned to him, appreciating his compassion. "He did," she acknowledged quietly. She straightened up in her chair and wiped tears from her cheeks.

Julia looked at her with anxious concern. "Mom, what's going on?"

Amelia gave Julia a weak smile and glanced inclusively to Lucca. "I'm okay," she assured them. "Life's just been a little too real lately." Their worried expressions prompted her to continue. "Which means I'm very tired. It's been a really full day, and I need to go to the castles early tomorrow. Let's go home."

* * *

The living room was almost dark when they arrived home, and Amelia moved through the dim light to turn on a lamp. "I'm going to say goodnight and leave you two to visit," she said to Lucca and Julia who lingered by the door, still looking worried. "Don't worry about me, I just need a good night's sleep," she insisted. She smiled, blew them a kiss and headed to her room.

"Goodnight Mom," Julia called after her. "Sweet dreams."

Not tonight, Amelia thought as she dropped her bag on a chair in her bedroom and walked into the bathroom to splash cold water on her face and neck. She needed sleep, not dreams. As she changed and crawled into bed she let the events of the day run through her mind, reminding herself there was nothing more to be done until tomorrow. She set the alarm to be sure she'd wake early to meet George, and turned out the light. Moonlight filtered into the room through the sheer curtains, and she glanced toward the window for a moment. She could see how beautiful the night sky was and breathed deeply, lingering with the view, thinking of George. She rolled onto her side and closed her eyes. Thoughts slipped away as the quiet whirring movement of the ceiling fan relieved the still air, and accompanied her into sleep.

* * *

The morning air felt cooler than it had in days, almost refreshing as she crossed the road to the ball field. She saw George walking toward her, arms full of grocery bags. She took one, noticing how tense he looked.

"It's cooler this morning," he commented, stepping onto the ball field.

"Finally. How are you doing?" she asked, keeping pace with him.

"Tired. I've been thinking about Jack and didn't sleep much," he responded.

"I was talking with Joe and Sarah at the café last night. They think he'll be passing soon George," she said with compassion.

"I know," he said, "that's what I was thinking about."

Nicia was sitting on her porch as they walked into the backyard of the castles. She had a bowl of green beans in her lap and was snapping them into smaller pieces and putting them in another bowl on the table beside her. "Good morning," she greeted them. "It's good to have the cooler air to start the day. A nice change," she said, smiling.

"It is a nice change," Amelia agreed, returning Nicia's smile.

"We've some groceries for you," George said, nodding toward the bag Amelia carried. "Shall we put them in the kitchen?"

"You go ahead Amelia," Nicia said, "just put them on the table. Thank you."

Amelia went into the house, and Nicia stopped what she was doing, looking intently at George.

"You've got to accept it and not worry George," she said. "We all have a time to go."

He nodded acknowledgement as Amelia came out onto the porch.

"How are you doing Nicia?" she asked.

"Not a worry for me," she replied. "I'm doing well like the others. They'll be out here in the garden soon. Sam and Phil have gone with Ted and Ricco, but maybe you could check on Lucianna Amelia, she was worried last night. George,

92   *E.G. Brook*

maybe you check on Jack," she suggested, looking at him compassionately. "It will be alright."

Amelia looked from Nicia to George, realizing they'd been talking about Jack. She watched silently as George turned and walked along the row of houses to Emma and Merle's, dropping a bag of groceries in a porch chair there, walking further to Joe and Sarah's and leaving another on their small table. He walked back to Jack's, opened the screen door and went inside with the last bag.

"Let him be Amelia," Nicia said. "He's had this trouble since Michael died, he needs to make peace with death. You go to see Lucianna, she needs to know there's no more she can do."

Lucianna burst onto her porch in her nightdress as Amelia walked along the row of houses. "I slept late," she said anxiously. "I was up into the morning with Jack, and then Nicia sat with him."

"George is with him now," Amelia said, stepping onto the porch and opening the screen door. "Let's go inside so you can dress," she encouraged. Lucianna moved toward the door, hesitating before going through, looking toward Jack's. "There's no more you can do Lucianna," Amelia said, gently placing her hand on Lucianna's back and guiding her inside. "You gave him the love and care he needed most." Lucianna stepped inside and Amelia followed. The screen door swung shut behind them.

* * *

Amelia walked home on her own, crossing the ball field with quiet resignation. Grief hung heavily with her, yet she was grateful Jack's suffering had ended. She felt little interest in planning activity for the day, and was glad the house was quiet when she reached home. The smell of coffee Lucca had made drew her to the cupboard to take out a mug and fill it.

Hunger moved her to the fridge for a carton of eggs, which she placed on the counter. She sipped coffee as she prepared scrambled eggs, and was putting bread in the toaster when Julia sleepily came into the room, wearing an attractive calf length cotton dress.

"Good morning," Amelia said, smiling for her daughter. "That's a lovely dress."

"A present from David," Julia said with affection. "Celebrating our news."

"What news?" Amelia asked.

Julia smiled but didn't respond, instead going to the cupboard and opening the door.

"Coffee's gone," Amelia stated. "Would you like me to make more?"

"No thanks," Julia answered. "I'll have water." She got herself a glass and filled it from the covered pitcher on the island counter. "You're back from the castles already," she noted, a little surprised.

"Yes," Amelia responded quietly. "Jack passed away early this morning."

"Oh Mom," Julia said with empathy.

Amelia smiled slightly, honoring Jack in her heart, easing the pain. "He was a kind man. He'll be missed."

The toaster popped up. Amelia took the toast and put it on a plate, buttering it as she continued. "Nicia and George are taking care of arrangements. Nicia thought it best if I came home, and I agreed with her." She handed the toast to Julia, and a plate of scrambled eggs.

"Isn't this yours?" Julia asked.

"I can make more," Amelia said. "Have a seat." She cracked a couple of eggs into a bowl and whipped them while Julia sat herself at the island counter. "No more evasion. Tell me your news," Amelia insisted.

Julia grinned. "After you told me about owning the

orchards I talked with David," she mentioned, keeping her excitement in check, "and we're considering moving back here."

"Julia!" Amelia exclaimed, in the midst of pouring the beaten eggs into the pan. She set the bowl down and turned to Julia expectantly. "Are you two serious about this?"

"Yes. Surprising I know," Julia admitted. "David wants to contract as an architect rather than work for a firm, and is already operating out of a home office. His work is known, and his reputation solid. He believes he can have a broader scope of clients working on his own, and travel for meetings when needed. It would give us more flexibility in choosing a home location. Being here would be possible." She paused, watching Amelia lift the pan from the stove and sweep the scrambled eggs onto a plate. "I've been thinking of making a change too," she continued. "I've been teaching at the college for several years now, and I'd like to get back into creating my own art. Maybe aim at opening a small studio gallery someday," she said hopefully. Amelia smiled and carried her breakfast around the island to sit next to Julia. "You're not saying anything," Julia stated, watching her.

"I'm listening," Amelia confirmed, smiling.

"We've also been talking about having kids, and we'd like to raise them in the country, relatively speaking," Julia declared. "Which is another reason for wanting to be back here," she added, pausing as she watched Amelia eat. "Mom?" she said, wanting her full attention.

"I'm listening baby," Amelia said, turning to her.

"I'm pregnant."

Amelia froze for an instant in astonishment. She shrieked with joy and jumped up, hugging Julia tightly. She was speechless.

"You're still not saying anything," Julia said, laughing.

"I'm delighted!" Amelia declared. "Overjoyed! Beyond

words," she exclaimed, releasing Julia. "When is the baby due?" she asked eagerly.

"Mid - February," Julia responded.

Amelia sat down again, happily caressing her daughter's hand as she spoke. "I couldn't be happier Julia. Have you decided when you want to be back here?"

"Before the baby's born if we can," Julia stated. "Lucca was talking about Will Trumble planning a residential development, and I'm interested in finding out more about that. Maybe that will give us an option for a new house, with office space and room to grow."

Amelia's smile faded, but she remained silent.

"Mom, you're looking at me funny. What's happening?"

"Long story sweetheart, for another time," she commented. "Briefly, Will's interested in some of my land for those developments. I got copies of his proposals yesterday. I'm undecided about his ideas and not looking to sell any land. I need to review what he's put forward."

"Oh," Julia commented, her enthusiasm subdued.

"I've asked the town Council to bring the proposals to the community for feedback, and was planning to draft an opinion survey to present at the Council meeting later this afternoon."

"Could we do that together?" Julia asked. "Maybe I can help."

"I thought you were planning to spend time in the vineyards."

"Tomorrow morning when I can get up early and go with Lucca. I was too tired today."

"Mmm," Amelia acknowledged. "I remember sleeping a lot in early pregnancy."

"So I'm discovering," Julia said, wrinkling her nose with mixed feelings about the need.

"You'll adjust," Amelia said, giving her daughter a

reassuring smile. She sipped her coffee as Julia ate, imagining her with a baby. The thought made her chuckle. Julia had always loved being the baby in the family; she was going to be making a lot of adjustments.

Amelia brought her attention back to the day. "I'd love your help with the proposals," she confirmed. "Let's get started right after breakfast."

"Great," Julia agreed, happy to be included in her mom's activity.

The task was more challenging than either of them anticipated. Review of the proposals went relatively smoothly, yet identifying key components and drafting questions for the survey was difficult, and took them into early afternoon. When they finally finished Julia was ready for a nap, and Amelia had barely enough time to change for her meeting with the Council.

Chapter 7

Amelia didn't see Will's truck in the Municipal Centre parking lot, and decided to check in with George before her meeting. She found him in his office, sitting at his desk writing on a piece of paper. She knocked at the door and he looked up with surprise.

"Amelia," he said. "I wasn't expecting to see you."

"I thought I'd stop by and see how you are, before meeting with the Mayor," she explained. She entered his office and sat opposite him. He looked fragile, as if grief would overtake him at any moment. "I've been thinking of you," she added, feeling helpless when she saw tears come to his eyes. "Do you need to be here, at your office?" she asked with empathy.

"I'll be leaving soon," he said, noticing her eyes go to the piece of paper on his desk. "I'm just writing down some things to do for Jack. Legal stuff, notifications, and funeral arrangements."

She turned to the window, tears welling up in her own eyes. "It's hard," she said, turning back to him. "I can imagine how difficult this must be for you."

George met her gaze for an instant and quickly turned away. "I'm sorry. I'm barely keeping it together. I can't talk about it."

"We don't need to talk," she said, reaching across the desk and caressing his hand. "If I can help please come to me."

George was silent, unable to look at her. She stood, and stepped into the hallway.

"Amelia," George called. She looked back into his office. "It might take me awhile." She smiled gently and nodded understanding, wiping tears from her cheeks as she walked down the hallway to the meeting.

She entered the Council chamber somberly and took the vacant chair at the far end of the table. She was determined to avoid a confrontational meeting and smiled as she sat next to the only woman Council member, a former school friend of Julia's. She glanced around the table and noticed Will wasn't there. The other five Council members and the Mayor were watching her with grave expressions, which prompted her to speak.

"Good afternoon Kate," she said to the young woman. "Gentlemen," she added with a friendly nod in their direction.

"Mrs. Marin," said the Mayor hesitantly. "Shall I call you Mrs. Marin? Or would you prefer Ms. Quinn?"

"Now that we know both are the same person, I think it would be best to call me what you always have Dan, Mrs. Marin."

He looked relieved. "Thank you Mrs. Marin. Unfortunately Will Trumble is unable to join us due to a family matter. This special Council meeting was requested to discuss the development projects you and Mr. Trumble have brought to our attention, both involving land you currently own. Could we begin with a statement of your opposition?"

Amelia shifted in her seat, sitting forward. Opposition was not where she intended to begin. "Please allow me to begin by thanking each of you for accommodating this meeting today. I'd also like to note that collaboration between the

Council, Will Trumble and myself has been requested, to review and decide whether the projects go forward or are denied." Amelia paused to check the effect of her words on each of the Council members; they were reserved. She continued, "With regard to your question about the development projects, it's not a matter of opposition, it's a matter of conscience. If we look at the Creek Road project initially, the apartment complex proposal would provide housing for middle-income residents, which has merit in principle, though if carried out it would create inequity. Currently rental housing is priced very high, which is out of reach for these residents, and many others in our community. I've asked Mr. Trumble to consider where the people who live in the existing houses would live if the houses were demolished, as there is no low income housing in the area. I ask for the same consideration from the Council, and propose we put the question before the community."

"That's not our usual practice," Dan said.

"Perhaps it could be," Amelia stated.

The Council members were obviously uneasy with the suggestion.

"The second proposal is for development of a 27 acre parcel of land on Quince Road, to include 53 houses and a recreational park," Dan stated.

"That land is zoned for agriculture Dan, with a two acre per residence bylaw," Kate stated.

"Yes, I'm aware of that. The proposal also includes application for rezoning," commented Dan.

"On what grounds?" Kate asked, her voice rising.

"We're getting ahead of ourselves," Dan said. "Mrs. Marin would you please state your position on this proposal?"

"As mentioned, the land is zoned for agricultural use, and I believe it would be best used for that purpose. Will expressed his belief that residential development of the land would be prosperous for local businesses and attract new businesses to the area, encouraging town growth. I'm not aware that town growth is commonly considered beneficial. I suggest the question be put before the community."

"I can't honestly see how that could be done, and I'm concerned about setting precedent," said Dan.

"Perhaps a precedent that includes community consultation on community development could be a good step, rather than a concern," Amelia stated.

"Dan this could really open a can of worms," said Frank nervously, the Council member sitting on Dan's left. Dan quieted him, motioning with his hand for him to wait.

Amelia continued, "An outline of each proposal accompanied by an opinion survey could be electronically or physically sent to each household, specifying the date for completion and return. Review of responses received could indicate the following step to be taken, perhaps a public meeting." She paused, providing opportunity for the members to speak. No one did, and she continued. "The opportunity to express views and hear the views of others, without argument or forcing opinion, could assist the community to discover common ground, and where views differ. Views naturally vary among people, and they can be expressed and investigated without argument if people are willing to allow it, to give each other the courtesy of being heard."

The Council members sat silently.

"To use the Creek Road proposal as an example, what I'm describing is a way to explore the question of affordable housing for the current residents of the housing proposed for demolition. I believe it could assist us to find an equitable answer." She paused, looking from person to person. "An equitable answer is necessary," she emphasized, "for me to consider selling the land to Will in support of the project."

"Mrs. Marin I'm sure you're aware that your suggestion is unorthodox," Dan stated.

"New practices usually are, Mayor," Amelia noted.

Dan leaned back in his chair, perplexed.

Amelia leaned back and continued, "Before we go further, please acknowledge the request for collaboration between the Council, Will Trumble and myself. The suggestion to invite the community to share their views on these two development proposals depends on agreement to enter into that collaboration. The final decision on each proposal would be made by the three collaborating members, by agreement or majority vote."

She looked at two men talking quietly among themselves. They noticed and fell silent.

"I presently hold the reins on these projects, as I am the landowner," she stated. "I'm willing to release that position to work together with the Council and the developer, and jointly come to decision. I'm interested in investigating any benefit the developments Will's proposing might bring to the community, including the current occupants of the Creek Road houses. At the moment I'm aware of none," she noted, "and please don't tell me about economic growth, profits and jobs. This is not an economic growth issue, it's a human one."

The Council members sat speechless. Amelia waited a moment before continuing. "I have a sample of what an opinion survey could look like," she said, taking the folder containing the papers she and Julia had prepared from her cloth bag and placing it on the table. "An overview of a project introduces each of the two sections of the survey, followed by nine questions and a space for additional comment in each section. I leave it with the Council for review, revision, or use as members decide."

Kate looked at Amelia, smiling with open admiration as

she sat forward in her chair. "I make a motion that the Council members discuss Mrs. Marin's suggestions and request for collaboration," she said, "and a second meeting with Mrs. Marin and Mr. Trumble be scheduled."

"I second the motion," Dan said. "All in favor please raise your hand." All Council members raised their hands. "Thank you Mrs. Marin, we'll be in touch with you."

Amelia stood, feeling her body quiver with a release of tension. "Thank you for your time and consideration." She took a deep breath, exhaling slowly as she left the room.

* * *

Julia had dinner ready when Amelia got home, and was sitting at the table chatting with Lucca.

"Did you tell him the news?" Amelia asked smiling.

Julia grinned. "I did," she said. "He can't get his head around being Uncle Lucca."

"It makes me feel old," he protested.

"Lucca my love," Amelia said, putting her hand on his shoulder, "you are 37, and not growing younger." Lucca took her hand and pulled her around in front of him.

"I'm eternally young Mom," he said playfully.

Amelia chuckled. "Well, you'll be the first," she quipped, picking up a glass and pouring herself a drink of water from the pitcher in the center of the table.

Julia glanced at Lucca. "Come on Lucca, tell her," she urged.

Amelia stopped drinking, looking intently at the two of them. "Tell me what?"

Lucca smiled. "There's someone I'd like you to meet."

Amelia gazed at him with a gentle playfulness. "There is?"

Lucca chuckled. "Her name's Jasmine," he said, "and we talked last night about coming here together mid-August if that's okay with you."

Amelia leaned over and put her arms around his neck, hugging him. "How wonderful Lucca! Of course it's okay with me."

"Great," he said, embracing her hug.

Amelia caressed his back as she moved around him to sit across from Julia. "I need mom info," she stated, looking expectantly at him.

"He can tell you more while we eat," Julia informed them, getting up and bringing a large serving bowl of penne pasta with seasoned meatballs and tomato sauce to the table. She set it next to a bowl of green salad.

Lucca picked up the pasta dish and held it for Amelia. "Moms first," he stated, passing it to Julia with a grin after Amelia had taken a serving. Julia smiled, enjoying being an expectant mom. She helped herself to a modest portion. "*That won't make you strong,*" Lucca said, adopting his father's accent, and scooped another spoonful onto her plate. They laughed.

Amelia plied Lucca for details about Jasmine as they ate, learning she was Indo-Canadian, 29, worked as a physiotherapist, and they'd been introduced to each other by a mutual friend about seven months ago.

"She's beautiful, kind, and smart," Lucca concluded with obvious affection.

Amelia was pleased. "I'm looking forward to meeting her."

A flood of mixed emotions swept in, urging her move. She got up and went to the fridge, thinking to find something for dessert. Energy surged through her and she consciously deepened her breath, slowing down the exhale, realizing how much had happened in the day - Jack's passing, Julia's news of moving back and having a child, George's distress over Jack's death, the meeting with the Council, and now Lucca's news of meeting someone who'd touched his heart and was very likely coming into their lives. She realized her emotions were piling up with all she'd felt the previous day, and reassured herself that she was simply overwhelmed. The acknowledgement helped her focus her attention, and she opened the freezer, choosing a container of gelato and taking it to the table with a scoop she pulled from a drawer. Currents of sorrow and joy swirled within her, but the overwhelming anxiousness was beginning to dissipate. She sat down, looking to Lucca and Julia. "It's been an amazing couple of days."

"That's an understatement. You've got a lot going on besides breaking the news to us about owning the land, which was major," Lucca said with concern, noticing how her mood had shifted. "I don't think you expected we'd opt to be involved. Or that you'd be dealing with all the other stuff right now. Are you okay?"

"I'm okay," she assured him, recognizing she would be. Neither he nor Julia knew how deeply Jack's passing was affecting George, and how that was affecting her. She wished she could share their happy news with him, and perhaps briefly relieve his grief.

* * *

The rest of the weekend was filled with activity, the weather more livable at its seasonal norm. Julia felt conflicted when she went to the vineyards with Lucca. She'd had many happy times there with her father, but wasn't attracted to the kind of work involved, nor the unpredictability of the harvests. She realized her heart was more invested in the orchards; she felt able and willing to deal with the challenges. She commented on how difficult it must have been for her mom, managing it all since her dad passed. Amelia insisted it was second nature to her, and spent hours touring the Quinn land with Julia, helping her come to a better understanding of the extent of work and risk involved in owning and managing the orchards. Julia remained sincere in her interest to take on the responsibility if Amelia chose to pass the land to her. Lucca made it clear he would offer moral support, but his interest was with the vineyards and the possibility of establishing a winery. They spent Julia's last afternoon together at the lake, planning to walk over to the castles when they returned home. Julia was eager to share news of the coming baby, and Amelia wanted to invite everyone to dinner at the café before Julia flew home the next day.

* * *

The café was full when they arrived, except for the tables overlooking the vineyard Amelia had reserved. They were a large group, happy to be together celebrating Julia's news of the baby. Sarah joked about how old it made her feel. Hannah talked about the unexpected joy of sharing "firsts" with the baby, her favorite being the first time her daughter had heard water trickling over dishes in the sink – she'd listened so intensely. Joe joked about how active Julia was as a little girl, and wondered how she'd do keeping up with a 'live-wire' of her own. Amelia and Lucca laughed; Julia grinned.

Sam mentioned missing Jack, and Nicia told a story of when Jack had fixed the drain in her bathtub many years ago. Her youngest son wasn't yet in school, and had climbed into the tub to watch what Jack was doing. Jack had shown him every step he took and told him exactly how he would replace the drain. As he finished the work Jack had called to Nicia, asking what her son was saying to him in Italian. Her son had said, 'Buon lavoro,' Nicia told them, 'Good job.' They laughed, and Ricco raised his glass of wine to Jack, always alive in their hearts. Everyone raised their glass to the toast and drank together - wine, lemonade, iced tea, and water. There was more laughter with Sarah's mention of how Jack would have enjoyed the variety of beverages raised in his honor. Jack had been the most inclusive, Lucianna commented. His acceptance of people had been an inspiration, Ricco added.

Amelia grew quiet, thinking of George. Nicia seemed to sense her thought, sitting next to her, and gently touched her shoulder. "George couldn't bear to be here," she consoled her, "but he will be well again. Be patient Amelia. He's grieving what he couldn't grieve before. Now the loss of Michael is with him, as is the loss of Jack." Amelia put her hand on Nicia's, acknowledging the truth with a weak smile.

* * *

Amelia dreamt of her grandfather and Grace again, waking frightened with the emergence of the ocean. She went over the dream in her mind as she lay awake, wondering what it meant. Could San Francisco fall into the ocean? No. The tectonic plates in California didn't move in a way that would cause that to happen. It must be symbolic, but of what? The uneasy feeling persisted. At dawn she rose and went outside to the garden by the fountain, listening to the trickling water, watching the castles gradually light up as the sun rose behind her. She felt better with the sunrise, and realized she may never know what the dream meant. With resignation Amelia returned to the house and quietly crossed into the kitchen. She poured herself a glass of water and sat at the table as she drank, gazing out the window toward the castles.

"You seem lost in thought," Julia said, coming into the kitchen and pouring water for herself. "Are you thinking about the Council?"

"No," Amelia responded, "but I expect to hear from them

today." She took another sip of water and turned to Julia.

"What then?" Julia persisted, sitting beside her. "That faraway look meant something.'"

"I've been having the same dream almost every night for several weeks," Amelia confided. "Actually, versions of the same dream," she clarified, "and I don't know what it means."

"Maybe it's just a dream," Julia said casually.

"Not recurring like this. Some dreams are just biochemistry, maybe from late night eating. In other dreams it seems I'm trying to sort something out. With these dreams it seems something's being sorted out for me, or they're showing me something I need to understand."

"What do you mean, sorted out for you?"

"Something in them is actually going to happen, a dejá vu kind of thing," Amelia explained. "Since these dreams are about the past, that doesn't make sense. There must be something I need to understand. I have no idea what."

"Have you ever dreamt about something before it happened?" Julia asked with curiosity, getting up from the table and going to the fridge.

"I dreamt about my aunt's pregnancy when I was a teenager," Amelia stated simply. "It happened."

"That could be a coincidence. Your aunt having a baby doesn't seem unusual." Julia came back to the table with yogurt, cereal, two bowls and spoons.

Amelia smiled. "Well the details were. My aunt had just had a baby, and a difficult birth. In my dream the pregnancy and childbirth were the opposite. She felt well, and had an easy birth."

"Really?" Julia asked, intrigued.

"Really. The babies were less than a year apart." Amelia took the bowl Julia handed her and poured herself some cereal. "I remember my mother felt uneasy about my mentioning the dream to my aunt, which I can understand now, but at the time I didn't. I thought my aunt would want to know. I think she was stunned." Julia handed her yogurt, which Amelia took and scooped a heaping spoonful onto her cereal. "My mother told me later that my aunt had only just learned she was pregnant when I told her, and hearing about the dream actually helped her." She turned to Julia and shrugged. "Maybe that's why I had the dream, who knows?"

Julia was fascinated. "Do you have dreams come true very often?"

"No, there's only been a few."

"Well what's bothering you about the one you keep having now?"

"It seems to evolve, continuing to show me new things. Last night I was a young girl in San Francisco again, listening to someone speak in another language. My grandfather as a young man was with me, and he could hear what was said translated into English, but I couldn't. When I asked what was being said and he told me, I saw the words written on a page in a book, and one phrase was luminous, *'On the other hand, it is evident and true, though most astounding, that in man there is present this supernatural force or faculty which discovers the realities of things and which possesses the power of idealization...'*"

"What?!" Julia said with astonishment.

"Exactly, and I've seen more of that same passage in another version of the dream. There's always a little girl named Grace, and she and my grandfather walk away together and I'm left behind, unable to follow them or call out." She paused, putting her spoon in her cereal. "Last night, as once before, I saw Grace as a young woman go into a building. The building faded away and all I could see in every direction was ocean, with waves and whitecaps in the breeze. It frightened me, and I woke up."

"Why were you frightened?"

"I've no idea," Amelia declared honestly.

"It's so curious that you're having versions of the same dream," Julia commented, looking at Amelia intently. "Is this your real grandfather, or a grandfather in the dream?"

"My real grandfather. He came here from San Francisco in 1912, bought the first land and established the first orchards. I was very close to him."

"So he actually lived in San Francisco. I wonder if he really did some of the things you're seeing in the dream."

"I've been wondering that too," Amelia admitted.

"I've got lots of time, I can do some research when I get home. Since you were in a crowd maybe some big event happened in San Francisco in 1912. Write down the passage you saw written in the book, and I'll see if I can find anything online."

"Okay," Amelia said, feeling hesitant.

"Don't you want to?" Julia asked, noticing Amelia's hesitance.

"It makes it feel real," Amelia confided.

"Well maybe it is," Julia said lightly, and smiled reassuringly at her mom. She picked up the yogurt and scooped some onto her cereal.

Lucca came into the kitchen and checked for coffee. "Good morning moms," he said playfully.

Julia grinned. "Good morning Uncle Lucca."

Amelia's phone rang. She got up and moved to the counter, checking the screen. 'Town Council' she mouthed silently to Julia.

"Hello," Amelia said, answering the call. Lucca kissed her forehead as she listened, and she smiled at him, caressing his cheek. "Thank you, I'm glad to hear that." She listened again. "Returned in two weeks, okay." She paused, listening. "Yes, I can meet with the Mayor tomorrow morning at ten.

Good. Thank you."

She ended the call triumphantly. "The Council decided to collaborate, and use the project overview and survey as presented. It's being sent out to everyone in the community today with notice to complete and return it within two weeks. Will and I meet with the Mayor tomorrow morning to hear what else the Council has to say."

"Wonderful!" Julia agreed.

"I don't think Will's going to be there Mom," Lucca said. "His father's in a hospital on the coast, and Will's setting his mom up in an apartment."

"That explains why he wasn't there yesterday," Amelia acknowledged, moving back to the table. "It must be tough for him. I hope we can come to a workable decision on these development proposals."

Lucca came to the table with a bowl and spoon, sat down and poured himself some cereal. "Are you packed and ready to go?" he asked Julia. "Remember it takes an hour to drive to the airport."

Julia nodded. "We've got time to enjoy breakfast before we leave, not to worry."

* * *

Amelia fell asleep in the hammock while Lucca was gone. The sound of the water flowing over the stones in the fountain eventually stirred her, but she kept her eyes closed, lingering with the drowsiness. She barely noticed footsteps as they approached her, but wasn't surprised by Lucca's kiss on her forehead. She opened her eyes and smiled up at him.

"Julia's plane left on time?"

"It did, no problems. Traffic around the airport was a little crazy though."

"The Regatta happens this week," Amelia explained.

Lucca nodded. "I'm going to have dinner with Ned. He

still seems to think I have some influence with you, even though I've told him I'm not getting into it." He smiled. "Ned's okay when he's not trying to be Mr. Real Estate."

Amelia chuckled. "No doubt."

Lucca held the car keys up and jiggled them.

"Yes, take the Mustang. I'm planning on a quiet evening and going to bed early."

"Thanks," he said, giving her another kiss on the forehead. "See you tomorrow."

Amelia turned her head to the fountain, watching the water flow down and pool in the basin. The sound was soothing, but it didn't ease the loneliness she felt. She wasn't able to reconcile how much she missed George. It had been several days since she'd seen him, and she'd hoped the missing and worry would subside. Instead it was growing stronger. Nicia had assured her he was alright. She needed to believe that.

* * *

Lucca accompanied her to Jack's funeral, which was a short graveside service. The morning air was warm, the breeze light. Many attending had removed their hats, and held them in hand. Amelia's eyes roamed over those gathered, friends from the castles, crew from the orchards, the vineyards, and many community members. A wreath of grapevines lay across the centre of the wooden casket, and Amelia rested her eyes there as Nicia began to speak.

"Several years ago Jack gave me a note describing how he wanted his burial to be," Nicia said with affection. "Graveside, simple, he hoped with fond memories," she relayed, projecting her voice over the crowd as she could. "Jack chose one passage to be read, taken from a prayer he heard at the funeral of a dear friend, the elder Michael Quinn."

Amelia looked up with surprise. She remembered very

little of her grandfather's funeral.

"I'll read that passage now," Nicia said with a soft tone to her voice she hadn't heard her use before.

Amelia intuitively closed her eyes as she listened to Nicia read, feeling the breeze caress her skin and draw her hair away from her face. The words reverberated remembrance.

> *"O my God, Thy Trust hath been returned unto*
> *Thee. It behooveth Thy grace and Thy bounty*
> *that have compassed Thy dominions on earth and*
> *in heaven, to vouchsafe unto Thy newly*
> *welcomed one Thy gifts and Thy bestowals, and*
> *the fruits of the tree of Thy grace!"*

The chirping call of a golden eagle filled the silence as Nicia paused, and Amelia opened her eyes to look up. As Nicia continued reading she watched a lone eagle circle overhead on a wind current that dipped and rose above them.

> *"Powerful are Thou to do as Thou willest, there*
> *is none other God but Thee, the Gracious, the*
> *Most Bountiful, the Compassionate, the Bestower,*
> *the Pardoner, the Precious, the All-Knowing."*

A second golden eagle joined the first as Nicia finished reciting the passage, both carried away by the wind. Amelia looked to the others, wondering if anyone had noticed. Joe, Sarah and George had heard the call and were watching the eagles drift beyond the trees.

* * *

The next few days were spent with Lucca and Ricco, hearing their ideas for the vineyard and evaluating the current crop, looking at the proposed location for a winery and determining what financial investment would be needed. She was open to the changes and had the financial resources to invest in the winery, but she wasn't sure of the timing. Something was lingering in the back of her mind, holding her back. All she could understand was that something else was going to change, outside of her influence, and she needed to wait. Perhaps the results of the survey would indicate people were in favor of Will's developments, or perhaps the Council's reluctance to hold a public meeting would block reaching a decision. In the follow-up meeting with the Mayor it was confirmed that Will had gone out of town again. She felt compassion for Will and his family, and confused about how to move forward. Perhaps that confusion was spilling over into her consideration of timing for the winery.

Lucca returned to the coast at the end of the week, and Amelia found herself adjusting to his absence. It didn't take long to embrace the company of someone she loved, but it did take a day or two to become comfortable being on her own again. She occupied her weekend by searching for ways to amend the development proposals that might make Will's projects viable, particularly considering those who lived in the castles.

* * *

Amelia rose Monday morning with a feeling of restlessness that drove her outdoors. The plants needed water, she reminded herself, turning on the tap and pulling the hose across the lawn with a sense of purpose. She was fully aware the task was a distraction, not a remedy.

Sarah's arrival made the difference, the sight of her strolling up the driveway was a welcome one. Amelia stopped watering and dropped the hose to the ground.

"Hi Sarah," she said, walking toward her friend with a

broad smile. "Thanks for bringing the vegetables over." She took the basket Sarah handed her and matched her pace for the rest of the walk up the driveway.

"Nice to get out for a walk," Sarah said. "We've been staying close to home and the café in the heat, but it's getting to be too much sitting around. Joe's eager to fish, but what fish would come out of the water in this heat," she said, laughing at her joke.

Amelia chuckled. "Then I won't ask you to sit and visit, but I'd love your company."

"Here, let me water," Sarah suggested and walked over to the hose, picking it up. "You've probably got something else you're planning to do."

"I wish I did," Amelia said. "I'm feeling a bit lost with Lucca back on the coast. It always takes me a day or so to adjust to being on my own again, but with other things going on it's taking longer."

"You're missing George," Sarah acknowledged, sweeping the flow of water over the flower bed.

"I am," Amelia admitted, finally acknowledging the vulnerability she was feeling that had been plaguing her all morning. Sarah nodded with understanding and peacefully continued to water the garden.

"I'll take these inside and get us something to drink," Amelia said, responding to the need to do something. She climbed the stairs and went into the house while Sarah moved along the flower bed. Amelia returned with iced tea and banana bread on a tray.

"Come on Sarah, force yourself to sit," she called, walking around to her backyard and setting the tray on the small table. Sarah smiled, dropping the hose to join Amelia by the fountain. She sat in a lawn chair near the table, across from Amelia.

"You need to talk," she stated, looking into Amelia's eyes.

Amelia chuckled. "You've always been able to read me, ever since I was in high school."

"I understood. I was only a few years older than you, Joe and I marrying young and coming here. You and I have been sisters a long time," she said, and reached for a piece of banana bread. "Joe and I waited so long to have kids, working, you and I even had our kids together. It was good for the kids, having friends close by." She put a piece of banana bread in her mouth, chewed and nodded approval. "I won't ask if you baked this," she teased.

Amelia laughed. "Why would I bake when I have a café and employee staff who are excellent bakers?" She took the other piece of banana bread from the plate, broke off a piece and put it in her mouth. "It is good," she agreed, and chuckled. She felt so comfortable in Sarah's presence. "I've always been grateful for our friendship, for our kids having each other," she said sincerely. "Though you're much wiser than I am," she added, "you see things in me I don't see myself."

Sarah laughed. "I don't know how wise I am. You're like a chameleon Amelia, what you experience is easy to see in your face."

"To your eyes maybe," Amelia acknowledged. She hesitated to say more.

Sarah didn't hesitate. "So what's bothering you?"

"I'm worried about George," Amelia confided. "I haven't heard from him since Jack's death. He was with you at the funeral, is he okay?"

Sarah nodded. "He's okay," she affirmed.

"Have you seen him since the funeral?" Amelia asked.

"At the café. I think he's staying away from the castles. He still avoids his grief."

Amelia sat back in her chair, dismayed. "What am I going to do?"

Sarah looked at her with quiet certainty. "Wait," she replied. "That's your job now. Especially with the closeness you've allowed yourself to feel with George. This is George's work, let him find his way."

"How did you know what happened with George?"

Sarah smiled. "I could see it in your eyes."

"Sarah, you amaze me," Amelia said with heartfelt honesty.

Chapter 8

As the days passed it became more and more difficult for Amelia to ignore her longing to see George. It had been over three weeks since Jack's passing. She moved into her bedroom wrapped in a towel, refreshed by the shower after cleaning Jack's house with Emma and Sarah all morning. She felt distracted as she searched her closet for something to wear, and simply grabbed a light cotton shirt from a hanger and capris from a shelf. She wondered about arranging to see George before her afternoon meeting with the Mayor, but her gut told her no.

The gut instinct was accurate; George wasn't in his office when she arrived at the Municipal Centre. She continued down the hall and walked through the open door into the Mayor's office. This time Will was present.

"Please sit down Mrs. Marin," Dan said as she entered his office, indicating the chair next to Will. She seated herself, noticing Dan looked determined. Will looked tired. "Mr. Trumble has asked that this be a short meeting if possible. Council has reviewed the survey results, and if you're in agreement I'll move directly to the Council's report."

"Please do," Amelia agreed.

"The percentage of survey completion was quite high, 87% were submitted by the return date, and Council accepted another 2% received the next business day," Dan said. "Responses were tallied by the number of checks per category for each of the nine questions, totals calculated and converted to percentages, which is the value used in the Council's report. I have a copy for each of you." He handed each of them a several page document. "If you would please take a moment to review the percentages associated with each response, together we can consider any questions or comments you may have."

Will glanced through the pages of the report and looked toward Dan. "I'll need more time to review this properly and give it consideration. I have no comments to make at the moment," he said, hesitated, and added, "other than it seems the survey was a good idea."

"Mrs. Marin?" Dan asked.

Amelia lifted her head from reading the document. "I can see some trends in the responses, and agree with taking more time to review the report. I have no questions. However, I am interested in Council's recommendations for taking this process further."

"Revisions to the development proposals, or recommendation for their withdrawal, can be submitted by any of the three parties, meaning yourself, Mr. Trumble, and the Council, within 10 business days. A public meeting has been tentatively scheduled for the following Saturday at 7pm in the Community Hall. If submissions result in withdrawal of the development proposals, that meeting will be cancelled. If the public meeting goes ahead, a final meeting between yourself, Mr. Trumble and the Council will take place during the following week, at the regular Council meeting on Wednesday at 7pm. A decision to approve or deny the proposals will be made at that time."

"Thank you," Will said as he rose and extended his hand to Dan, who shook it. Amelia rose from her chair and looked at Will as he turned to leave. He hesitated, but remained silent.

"I'm glad you were able to make it today Will," she said with compassion. "I hope you can get some rest." He nodded slightly and left.

Amelia walked down the hallway and glanced into George's office. He wasn't there. She walked further to Steve's office, and lightly knocked on his door.

Steve turned his head from his computer. "Hi Amelia," he said, and smiled.

"Hi Steve. Have you seen George today?" she asked. "I was hoping to catch him after my meeting with the Mayor."

"He was in briefly this morning," he responded. "I expect he'll be back near the end of the day, that's his usual routine."

"Thanks," she said.

"I'll let him know you dropped by," Steve commented. Amelia smiled weakly, and left.

The heat that greeted her outside the air conditioned building was expected, but how upset she felt with being unable to see George unnerved her. She quickly crossed the parking lot to her convertible and drove to the lake, parking in the shade of a large maple tree. With one hand she slid the scarf from her hair and put it in her cloth bag, with the other she picked up the towel she'd left on the passenger seat.

An emotional eagerness propelled her out of the car and across to the shade trees at the edge of the sand. She kicked off her shoes, dropped the bag and towel on the sand and ran into the water, moving continually deeper until she felt the buoyancy support her. The surface of the lake broke cleanly as she dove down into its cool embrace. She came up briefly for air, and dove again, and again, determined to free herself from the insistent feelings of vulnerability and loneliness. Finally attaining a sense of calm, she swam toward the dock,

E.G. Brook

took hold of the ladder and pulled herself out of the water. She was breathless, but relieved, and hoped it would last. She leaned back on her hands and closed her eyes, raising her face to the sun.

"Oh George," she quietly lamented, "I'm not good with patience."

* * *

Hot and weary, George walked into his office and took off his hat, dropping it on a shelf. He flopped into his chair, glad it was nearly the end of the day. Sleepless nights weren't giving him much energy for work or anything else.

Steve stopped at his door as he was passing. "Amelia was just here."

"Looking for me?" George asked.

"No, meeting with Dan. Will was here too. There's been a lot of response to the survey about Will's development projects."

"That's good," George commented.

Steve hesitated a moment, trying to read George's flat expression. "You know George, you ought to go and see her. You're getting nowhere fast dealing with this on your own, and she's too fine a lady to ignore."

"I know," George replied, putting his elbows on the desk and dropping his head into his hands, closing his eyes.

"See her soon," he heard Steve say, followed by his footsteps going down the hall.

* * *

Amelia arrived home at dusk, having stopped by the café for dinner and a visit with Lucianna. They'd met to discuss the steady increase in clientele and consider hiring more staff, which was overdue. She was fortunate to have

Lucianna managing the café, Amelia realized as she climbed out of her car. She'd been distracted from the business for several weeks.

The evening was beginning to cool off and she walked through the garden into the backyard to enjoy it, knowing it would still be hot inside. As she rounded the corner of the house she stopped short; George was lying in the hammock. She smiled, and quietly drew nearer. He was asleep, dressed to visit in clean, casual clothes. She wondered how long he'd been there and sat nearby, lingering in case he woke up. The garden's night sounds and George's regular breathing relaxed her, and she realized it was the first time in a long time that she felt as peaceful as she did. Perhaps it was the same for him. She rose quietly, not wanting to disturb him, and went into the house.

George woke early the next morning to the sound of a truck driving by on the road. He opened his eyes and recognized where he was. Quickly swinging his legs out of the hammock he sat up, realizing he'd been asleep since early evening the night before. Amelia came around the corner of the house, a welcome sight in her summer dress, her hair swept up off her neck and held with a scarf, the length falling. He liked it like that.

"Good morning," she said quietly, approaching him.

"Good morning," he said, unsure of what else he would say.

She held his gaze for a moment in the silence, then smiled and turned toward the house. "Come inside, I'll get you some breakfast."

George followed her inside.

"You know where you can clean up," she said casually, moving across the living room into the kitchen. "Let me know if you need anything."

He disappeared down the hall without a word.

She placed a glass of water and a mug of coffee on the table, putting a small pitcher of cream within easy reach. George came into the kitchen looking refreshed, hair combed and damp around his face. She'd never seen him unshaven, and wrinkled her nose a little as he approached her.

"What?" he asked.

She swept her hand over her cheeks and chin, and chuckled. "You have a new look."

He smiled self-consciously and reached for her, drawing her close and nesting his face in her hair. Emotion overwhelmed him, and his eyes filled with tears. "I'm sorry," he said quietly, more surprised than she was when the tears broke loose.

Amelia silently held him, caressing his back and resting her head against his chest. His body shuddered as he wept, and she drew him closer, closing her eyes and companioning his grief. He gradually grew calmer and the tension in his body began to ease. She lifted her head, gazing at him tenderly, wiping tears from his cheeks with her fingertips. She kissed his cheek lightly. "Breakfast," she whispered, and gently moved back from their embrace.

He moved to the counter and wiped his eyes and nose with a tissue, tossing it in the garbage under the sink. He crossed to the table and picked up the glass of water, taking a long drink.

"Are you working today?" she asked, choosing two kinds of cereal from a cupboard and taking them to the table.

"No," he said, apprehensively turning to her. "I've taken the day off. I'd like to spend it with you." He worried that she'd stepped away from the relationship because of his absence, and looked to her for assurance.

She recognized his need. "I was hoping you'd say that," she said, her smile assuring him she was still with him.

With a rush of relief George pulled her into his arms,

kissing her with a longing he'd been afraid to feel.

Amelia's cell phone rang. George stepped back from their embrace; Amelia moved forward and kissed him again, sliding her hand down his arm as she moved away. She crossed to the island counter and with a brief glance at the phone knew it was a call she wanted to take. George sat down at the table.

"Hi Lucca," she said with enthusiasm, "are you calling to tell me what day you and Jasmine will be arriving?" She listened and chuckled. "Mother's intuition. That's good timing, there'll be a public meeting about Will's projects that Saturday evening. Julia and David might be coming then too." She listened. "Okay, renting a car's great. I'll expect you around six." She looked at George as she listened, and smiled. "Guest room for Jasmine, not a problem, you know I have lots of room." She listened again. "You're welcome to stay as long as you like." She walked over to George and stood beside him, resting her arm across his shoulders. "He's here now, I'll tell him. 'Bye." She touched the screen to end the call and looked down at George. "Lucca has met someone special and is bringing her here to meet me and visit the vineyards. He wants you to meet her too."

George wrapped his arms around her waist. "I'm guessing her name is Jasmine," he said, smiling. "Imagine Lucca getting serious." His smile lessened and he glanced at her phone. "How about turning the phone off?"

Amelia gently touched his cheek, seeing the fatigue in his face that testified to his state over the past few weeks. "Fair enough," she said, and kissed the top of his head. She turned the phone off as she crossed to the island counter, putting it in her cloth bag. "Done," she declared, and went to the cupboard for bowls.

"I can see how this is going to go," he teased. "You'll win your way with an agreeable kindness I can't resist."

Amelia turned to him with a serious expression and spoke with a quiet calmness. "There's no battle of wills between us George, don't take us there."

He looked at her with surprise. "Sorry, couple stereotype," he said apologetically.

"I know," she acknowledged with a slight smile. "Let's watch out for that."

* * *

When he returned to work, George realized the shift in relationship with Amelia had quickly become common knowledge.

"George," Steve called to him as he headed to his office. "Got a minute?"

George stopped and backed up a few steps, standing in Steve's doorway.

"The Council sent me a copy of their revision suggestions for Will's projects, and Will's been in talking to me about his plans a few times, but I haven't heard anything from Amelia. Do you know if she's submitting anything? The deadline's tomorrow."

George smiled. "I don't have an inside track," he stated. "Call her."

Steve shrugged and picked up the phone.

George headed toward his office. Dan stopped him in the hallway. "Do you know if Amelia's sending us any revisions on Will's project proposals George? We haven't heard."

George grinned. "I suggest you call her Dan," he replied, and continued on to his office, manoeuvering around the desk and sitting down. He wondered if Amelia was fielding George questions.

* * *

Amelia was in her kitchen with the phone on speaker, talking with Julia about revision of the development proposals. "My thought about the Quince Road property is to offer 20 acres for sale, and keep seven acres for our use in the future. Conditions of the sale would take into account survey results, specifically zoning remaining as is, meaning the land couldn't be subdivided under two acres. That could give Will 9 housing sites, and land for roads."

"That's a huge drop from 53 houses," Julia noted.

"And 9 more than 0," Amelia pointed out.

"Okay, so what about Creek Road? I'm thinking it's time for the castles to be replaced."

"No, the castles are well built, and they're subsidized by Quinn Orchards. None of the residents pay rent. They pay for their utilities directly to the utility companies, as we all do."

"Mom! How have you managed to do that?"

"Easily, it's always been that way. The cost of building them was covered long ago, and maintenance is covered by a fund my grandfather set up for that purpose. The fund grows more than it's needed, so there's never been a problem."

"Wow," Julia commented, "nobody does that anymore."

"Too bad they don't," Amelia stated.

"Well how are you ever going to replace that?" Julia questioned. "It makes taking those houses down a completely different issue."

"I've only had one idea, a barter agreement. The land and houses in exchange for seven, three bedroom units in the new buildings. Those units become the property of Quinn Orchards as the houses currently are."

"What about selling the land and buying seven units?" Julia suggested.

"That wouldn't be as advantageous for either party. More money would go to third parties in each transaction."

"Do you think the land is worth seven units?" Julia asked.

"It's not only the land Julia, it's also seven houses on the land. Will may want to tear them down, but they're completely livable."

"I wonder what everyone who lives in the castles would want."

"I'm hoping we'll find that out at the public meeting," Amelia said.

"Well as your sounding board I think the idea of a barter exchange is a good one, and worth putting forward."

"Good. I'd better go and draft a letter for the Council. I've already had two calls asking if I was planning to make a submission. I appreciate hearing your thoughts, thanks Julia."

"Mom wait," Julia interrupted. "David and I decided we do want to be there at the same time as Lucca and Jasmine. That will give us a chance to meet her. Our plan is to stay for about a week, so we can look at houses for sale in the area."

"That sounds wonderful," Amelia agreed. "I'd love it."

"Okay," Julia happily acknowledged. "We're going to rent a car at the airport, we'll be doing a lot of driving around. I'll let you know what time we'll be arriving once I book flights."

"Thanks baby, talk soon."

"Wait," Julia interrupted again. "I found something online that might be related to your dream."

"Could we save it until you're here? I've got to get this proposal written and submitted."

"Okay. 'Bye Mom."

Amelia ended the call and headed to her room to draft the revision letter. She was a little curious about what Julia had discovered, but could wait to find out.

* * *

Amelia received a call from Dan the next morning, just

before noon. Three revisions had been submitted in support of the projects, and the public meeting would go ahead the following Saturday at 7pm. Dan asked if she would chair the meeting, noting that she seemed to have an idea of how to handle such an event. She agreed, not bothering to tell him she'd only had one similar experience, with a roomful of angry parents when Lucca was in elementary school. She completed the call and decided she'd focus on the intention of the meeting - to give people an opportunity to speak, and an opportunity to listen.

* * *

Ned and Will sat at a café table with the Council Report open before them, their empty lunch plates stacked to one side.

Will took a drink of coffee. "What do you think?" he asked Ned.

"I think the Council has probably come back at you with some serious revisions. Probably fewer houses and larger lots on the acreage, and townhouses on Creek Road. If you're lucky," Ned said. He flipped through the pages of the report. "You said Lucca mentioned Amelia's revision proposes a barter agreement, suites for land at Creek Road, and you don't want that. Have you come up with ideas for some low income rentals for the people living in the old houses?"

Will shook his head. "None. There's still a couple of days before the public meeting."

"I'd say that's your priority. Nothing will happen on Creek Road without that."

"Geeze," Will said exasperated, "I don't need this hassle right now."

Ned sat back in his chair, looking at Will. "You said the Mayor's asked Amelia to chair the public meeting, so you need an edge. What about beating them to the punch? Draw up a plan for townhouses and see how many you could fit in. Or better yet, make the whole Creek Road project subsidized housing and apply for funding."

"Are you serious?" Will asked with disbelief.

Ned shrugged. "It's worth a shot. No housing for those folks is a deal breaker."

Chapter 9

Another heat wave came in on Thursday with daily temperatures rising 10 - 12 degrees above seasonal. As people gathered for the public meeting Saturday evening the air had only cooled to the daytime norm, which was hot. There was no air conditioning in the community hall, and all doors were open wide. When Amelia arrived she thought it looked full, guessing there were close to 90 people present. By the time the meeting was about to start the crowd had increased to 150, many standing around the edges of the room and in the open doorways.

Amelia walked to the microphone set up at the front of the room. "Hello everyone. Can you hear me?" she asked, testing the connection. A few people nodded, the crowd quieted down, and a couple of men shuffled into seats at the back of the room. "I'm glad you're here," she said. "With it being such a hot night we're going to do our best to help keep you cool, in more ways than one," she added with a smile. A few people chuckled. "There are two water tables at the back of the room, and we encourage anyone who would like a drink of water before we begin to please raise your hand. These resourceful souls starting a water chain will pass one to you." Many hands went up and volunteers filled cups that were passed person to person along the rows. When everyone was settled again, Amelia returned to the microphone.

"Let's get started. Most of you know me, and for those who don't I'm Amelia Quinn Marin, associated with Quinn Orchards and Marin Vineyards. I've agreed to chair this meeting," she said, pausing while two men arrived and moved along the side of the room to seats near the front. "Response to the Council's opinion survey has been significant, and we thank all who participated. It's provided a lot of information for consideration, and tonight's meeting provides more opportunity to express your views." Amelia waited a moment while Lucianna came in a side door and found a spot to stand against the wall. "We also want to thank Ms. Ellis, the Mayor's Assistant, who will be taking minutes of tonight's meeting. You can rest assured the Council will have an accurate record of views expressed."

Amelia looked toward Will and the Council members seated on her left. They were watching her anxiously. She took a deep breath and focused on the crowd. "We're going to begin by stating a few ground rules, so everyone who would like to speak has the opportunity to be heard." There were murmurs in the crowd, and many watched her intently. She raised her closed hand above her head. "First rule," she said opening her hand and extending one finger, "is to listen when someone is speaking, rather than interrupting. Second rule," she added as she extended a second finger. "Once a comment has been made, consider it belongs to the group and can be openly discussed, rather than considering it to belong to the person who made it. All speakers are encouraged to give their best effort to hear and contribute to the discussion, without taking offense if someone disagrees, or trying to push their point of view." There were more murmurs among the people in the audience. "Third and final rule," she said, extending a third finger, "be courteous and caring in the manner with which you speak and listen, and be confident in your right to express your view. We're all on the same playing field." She lowered her hand. The crowd waited expectantly.

"The first development proposed is the building of Orchard Towers apartments on Creek Road, on the site where Quinn Orchards houses now stand. The second project is the residential development and re-zoning of 27 acres of vacant land on Quince Road. An overview of these projects was provided with the survey."

"We don't want any towers," shouted a man in the middle of the room. "It'll block our view of the orchards and that's the main reason we bought in the Creek subdivision."

Amelia held up her hand to stop further comments. "I appreciate that there are concerns, and we're here to hear them. Before we get to that part of the meeting, please be patient while the developer and land owner share their outlook on the impact of the proposed developments." She looked over the crowd, giving those who met her gaze a smile and nod of acknowledgement. "If you look around you'll see there are a lot of us here, and we need to agree on the rules and objective of the meeting to be able to carry on." She moved away from the mic while people talked amongst themselves, picked up a glass of water from the table near her and took a long drink before returning to the mic. The crowd grew quiet. "To restate the objective as described in the survey, our aim is to determine if the development projects will be beneficial for the community, as well as the developer and the land owner," she specified. "Keep that in mind. We need to keep ourselves focused, give our attention to finding solutions for concerns, and avoid conflict over personalities or viewpoints." There were murmurs throughout the crowd as people commented on what she'd said. "Will Trumble has reviewed the community feedback provided by the survey. Let's hear his comments on his projects, and any revisions made to his original plans."

She looked at Will and stepped to one side as he rose from his seat and stepped to the mic. He was nervous, but determined, and placed papers on the table beside him while referring to one he kept in his hand.

"With regard to the comment made earlier," he said, "Orchard Towers exterior will be attractively finished and will add to the view for anyone living in the Creek Road subdivision. The orchards will still be in view." Murmurs arose again in the crowd. Will shifted his stance and continued, "Presently there are seven old houses on Creek Road, which is still a dirt road. The Orchard Towers development will include paving the road, putting in sidewalks and creating underground parking for Towers residents. There will be two buildings, each three stories high."

"That's too high," the same man said. "People will be looking right into my backyard."

Amelia stepped up to the microphone. "Mr. Adams," she said with authority, "I'm asking that you focus on solutions, not problems. What solution could you suggest for your concern?"

"That the buildings be lower," he said.

"Duly noted, thank you. That will be brought forward for discussion following the presentations." She stepped back.

Will looked uncertain about her interjection, yet stepped up to the mic and continued speaking. "Each of the buildings will contain 10 rental units per floor, and offer a combination of studio units, one, two and three bedroom units. Interior finishing will include crown moulding in larger suites and hallways, elevator access, and laundry facilities in every apartment. The exterior will be finished with a neutral HardiePlank and professional landscaping." He stopped, looking expectantly at the crowd.

Amelia stepped forward to the mic. "Are there any questions?"

"What will the rents be?" a woman from the back called out.

Will stepped to the mic again. "The rents will be set at fair market value."

There were groans from the crowd, and an older man stood up. "Who's going to benefit from this build Will, other than yourself?" There were several chuckles.

"The benefit will be to the whole community," Will responded, "with increased housing to meet current and future needs."

"There aren't any current needs for rentals that many of us can't afford," a young man shouted.

Amelia stepped back to the mic and held up her hand. "We're answering questions at the moment, please hold your comments. The opportunity to express them comes right after hearing from the land owner." She lowered her hand and scanned the crowd, looking for the residents of the castles. She spotted Emma and Merle in the center of the crowd with Nicia. Ricco and Ted sat separately near a door. "Are there any more questions for Mr. Trumble?" she asked. No one responded.

"Then we'll move on," she stated. "I'd like to address you as the land owner of the site proposed for the buildings." Someone gasped, and a buzz of chatter rose and fell away. "As many of you know the Quinn family originally built the "old houses" we call the castles in the late 1940s, for workers who helped us in our orchards. They've been well maintained over the decades. The land on which they stand has also been developed to provide an organic vegetable market garden, which supplies produce for castle residents, Alessandro's Café, and is sold at the local farmer's market.

Sale of the land in order for the apartment complexes to be built would create loss of home for all residents, and in some cases loss of livelihood. That is unacceptable to me without those losses remedied."

She paused and looked over the crowd, she had their attention. "What we are here to investigate is how building the apartment complexes could be beneficial for the community, including those currently residing on the land, or if the proposal should be rejected. A decision to approve or deny the proposal will be made by the town Council, Will Trumble and myself, following consultation on the proposal documents and community input. Are there any questions?" People spoke amongst themselves, but none posed a question. Amelia removed the mic from the stand and held it in her hand, pacing a few steps before the crowd. "The floor is now open for your comments. Please remember the rules and objective guiding us."

Mr. Adams stood up. "As I said before, I bought my place for the unobstructed view and relative privacy. I don't want to see apartment buildings built. I also buy the produce grown in the Castle Garden and would like to keep doing that."

"You mentioned buildings be lower in height as a suggestion earlier. Do you see that as a possible solution that would make this development beneficial?" Amelia asked.

"No I don't," Mr. Adams responded. "That wouldn't provide places for those people to live, or a place to grow vegetables." He sat down.

Emma stood up. "The market garden provides us with our income," she said, "losing that is like losing any other job, and we won't have money to live on. If any change happens, the best one would keep the garden or offer another place where it could be."

"Do you have any ideas about such a place Emma?"

Amelia asked.

Emma hesitated, then spoke bravely. "I've been thinking about it since I first heard about the apartment project, and I thought maybe a community garden could be made somewhere. It could provide space for the market garden, and also for small gardens for people who want to grow a few things but don't have yards, like people who would live in the apartments." She paused. "But I really don't think apartments are the way to go," she added, and sat down.

"I feel that way too," called the woman who spoke earlier. "We need more affordable housing in the community, not more we can't afford."

"Do you have a suggestion?" Amelia asked.

"No," she stated, "but maybe someone else here does."

The young man who'd spoken earlier stood up. "So let's just scrap the idea of apartments, and think of what might make stuff affordable, like maybe having smaller living units and common spaces everyone shares. Like a retirement living idea, but for young families and single people. A couple of shared laundry spaces rather than laundry in every suite, and a larger shared indoor recreation space, and smaller living areas in each unit. Good outdoor space, stuff like that."

"How would that make living there more affordable?" Amelia asked, interested.

"It wouldn't duplicate stuff, which means less investment, less utility use, and less upkeep."

"Would you live in such a place?" she asked.

"Sure," he said exuberantly. "I mean if it was affordable it would be great. I hope I'll be able to move out on my own someday. People would have to want to get along, you know think of each other and not just themselves." He grinned and sat down.

The crowd was quiet for a moment, and Amelia scanned to

see if anyone wanted to speak. She saw George; he looked like he had something to say. He smiled, noticing her attention was on him, and stood up.

"I suggest any change be change to improve the housing situation on Creek Road, rather than for individual profit," he stated. "If profit is going to occur, let it be profit for all concerned, perhaps monetary for some, situational for others." He sat down.

"What about townhouses with small yards?" someone called out.

"I like the idea of a community garden," a young woman said, "and suggest rental units be priced so someone working in the orchards or vineyards around here could afford them. Maybe at one third of that kind of wage. That's what a lot of the work is in this area. Maybe live in them a long time if you wanted, and raise a family."

Amelia nodded her acknowledgement. "Would anyone else care to speak?" she asked.

"No," a man shouted from the back of the room. "The rules took care of everything I wanted to say." He and his buddies laughed.

Amelia looked to the town Council members seated on her left, and Ned Roberts seated at the back of the room. None signalled they wished to speak. She waited a moment longer. "Thank you. Will is there anything more you would like to say?"

Will took the mic she held out to him. "After reviewing the survey report I have considered revising the Orchard Towers apartments to subsidized rental units, and applying for funding in support of that possibility. Would that address some of the concerns mentioned?"

A few people shouted, "Yes!" and several applauded. Mr. Adams waited for the crowd to quiet down. "Some, but not all concerns," he said.

"Thank you," said Will. "I'll take that into consideration."

Amelia stepped up beside him and leaned toward the mic. "Now please tell us about the Quince Road property Will."

Will looked over the crowd. "Survey results clearly indicate the Quince Road development as proposed would be unfavorable for a majority in the community. Intention to submit a revised proposal that suggests a smaller development has been mentioned to Council. Details have yet to be worked out," he concluded and handed the mic to Amelia.

"Are there questions or comments regarding a development on Quince Road?" she asked.

Mr. Adams stood. "I don't think we need that development at all, we've got houses for sale. I don't want to see a development that's going to attract people to the area that won't appreciate the lifestyle here, and want to make more changes. We're an agricultural community with a small service town. That's not what people looking for a view want," he stated and sat down.

"I don't think it hurts to consider a more residential than rural neighborhood. I'd like to see something developed on that land," said a middle-aged man standing by a side door.

An older man called out from the front of the room, "The density of housing is my biggest concern. There's a lot of infrastructure needed for that, sewer, water, utilities established up there. There aren't any other houses in that area. How's it going to affect things environmentally?"

A woman at the back of the room spoke. "I'm wondering how affordable those houses would be, if they'd be within reach of any locals who might want to move up there, or if they'd be high end houses to attract people up from the coast."

There was a lull in the comments. Amelia scanned the room to see if anyone was indicating they wanted to talk. A lot of people were fanning themselves in the heat. "Thank you for your comments, they've been noted and will be considered," she confirmed. "I realize the heat is difficult for all of us, so if there are no further comments, I'll ask the Mayor to close the meeting."

She turned to Dan, who looked surprised, but walked forward and took the mic she held out to him.

"Thank you all for coming," he said. "The Council will be meeting with Mr. Trumble and Mrs. Marin, and an announcement of the decisions made will be posted on the town website within the next two weeks. Have a good night."

People stood and slowly made their way out of the hall, some momentarily stopping to say hello to a friend, others standing in groups talking. Amelia turned to Will and the Council members, acknowledging the Wednesday meeting scheduled before saying goodnight. Will thanked her, and quickly headed toward Ned Roberts who stood by a back door. The Council members lingered, talking with each other.

Amelia looked around for George, spotted him by a side door and moved through the crowd toward him.

He smiled and put his arm around her shoulder when she reached him, walking with her toward the door. "Come on Madame Chairman, let's get out of this sauna and go to the lake."

"Sorry George," she replied, "Lucca and Jasmine just got in before the meeting, and Julia and David will have arrived by now. Come and visit."

"Sure," he agreed, and they stepped outside into the night air. Amelia saw Lucca and Jasmine standing by a tree to one side of the crowd, and headed toward them.

"That was interesting," Lucca said. "You showed a new side of yourself Mom."

"Maybe," said Amelia, smiling. She turned to Jasmine. "Jasmine, this is George, a dear friend of the family for many years. George, this is Jasmine, someone special to Lucca I'm eager to know."

Jasmine smiled with an open friendliness. "Happy to meet you George."

"Likewise Jasmine," George responded, noting the ease of her manner. "I hope you and Lucca enjoy your time here despite the heat."

Lucca smiled and put his arm around Jasmine. "I'm sure we will. She teases about being made for hot climates."

Amelia smiled. "Any advantage in the heat is a good advantage."

"Let's go home," Lucca suggested and started toward the parking lot.

"I'll give your mom a lift. We can meet you two back at the house," George said.

Lucca stopped and turned to them, studying them briefly. He smiled. "You two made the shift."

George grinned. Amelia smiled and put her hand on Lucca's back, steering toward the parking lot, caressing him as they walked.

"Speechless," Lucca teased. "That's a first."

Amelia chuckled, branching off with George toward his truck.

* * *

Julia and David were relaxing on the porch swing when they got home. "Hello!" Amelia called, climbing out of George's truck and hurrying up the stairs. They stood up and each gave her a hug.

"So good to see you David," Amelia said enthusiastically. "Julia baby, you're getting round," Amelia said joyously, gently rubbing her daughter's abdomen.

Julia glanced over at David. "There'll be a lot of this," she told him. David smiled his approval. "Hi George," Julia said as he reached the top of the stairs, "you remember David."

"I do," said George, nodding to him. "Good to see you both, and I'm happy to hear your news. Congratulations!"

Lucca and Jasmine joined them on the porch. "Hello you two," Lucca cheerfully greeted Julia and David, turning affectionately to Jasmine. "I'd like you to meet someone very special to me, Jasmine Bagai," he said, smiling broadly as he looked back to his sister. "Jasmine, this is my sister Julia, and her husband David."

Jasmine smiled confidently. "It's wonderful to meet you both, and congratulations on the pregnancy! I'm very happy for you."

"Now introductions are done we can relax," Lucca said, and guided Jasmine toward the wicker sofa. Julia rushed over and intervened.

"Not so fast big brother," she teased, and hugged them both. "We're delighted to meet you Jasmine."

George leaned back against the porch railing, and Amelia dropped into a wicker chair. "What a night, I'm glad to sit down."

"Can I get you something to drink Mom? I noticed a pitcher of iced tea in the fridge," Julia said.

"Oh, please," responded Amelia. "Anyone else?"

Everyone raised their hand and Jasmine laughed. "I'll help you," she said to Julia and walked inside with her.

"She's lovely," Amelia said to Lucca. "I'm looking forward to getting to know her."

Lucca smiled. "You'll like her," he affirmed.

Julia and Jasmine came out with glasses of iced tea, serving each person individually. "I couldn't find the tray," Julia said to Amelia, "did you move it?"

"Maybe," Amelia acknowledged. "I honestly can't remember. There are too many things on my mind."

"I'll see if I can find it while I'm here," Julia said, smiling.

She sat down next to David, sipping her iced tea. "I'm going to say goodnight and head to bed after this," she informed them. "I've been feeling tired all evening."

"No nap this afternoon I bet," Amelia said playfully. "Baby making fatigue."

"You know I've noticed that ever since you mentioned it when I was here," Julia declared.

"Of course," Amelia teased. "I was right." Everyone laughed. Amelia looked to Julia. "It's normal during the first months of pregnancy, enjoy the rest," she encouraged.

George put his glass down on the coffee table. "Time for me to head home," he said, putting his hands on Amelia's shoulders and massaging them as he talked. "I'm hoping to convince your mom to come to the lake with me tomorrow afternoon. Would anyone like to join us?"

Lucca looked at Jasmine and she nodded yes. "Count us in," he said.

"We're touring the area and looking at houses in the morning. We could join you there when we're done," Julia said, and looked at David. "I'm guessing we'll want to cool down." David nodded.

"Good," George said, "I'll see you tomorrow." He gave Amelia's shoulders a gentle squeeze and left.

"That's my cue," Julia said, putting her glass on the coffee table. "Goodnight everyone." David got up and gave Julia his hand, she stood and nestled into his side. "What a gentleman," she teased.

David smiled. "Goodnight," he said, and they went inside.

Amelia rose and picked up some of the glasses, Jasmine quickly got up and helped her. Amelia smiled. "Thank you Jasmine. Come, I'll show you your room."

"I'll get the bags," Lucca said and headed down the stairs. He heard a car pull into the driveway behind him as he lifted the two small suitcases out of the trunk. He turned and saw

Ned getting out of his car. "Hey Ned, surprised to see you. I thought you and Will were heading to the coast right after the meeting."

"We're leaving tomorrow morning. Will's mom asked him to take some things to her from the house. He had to find them." Ned hesitated before continuing, "I came over to ask you something in person. Will's not sure he'll be back for the Wednesday meeting with your mom and the Council, and he's asked me if I'd sit in for him. Do you think they'd go along with that?"

"No idea."

"Any suggestions on how I should approach it?"

Lucca closed the trunk and picked up one of the suitcases, resting it on top of the other. "I don't think you should do anything, it's up to Will. From what I know about how things work in this town, which is little, I'd suggest Will call the Mayor at the beginning of the week and have a conversation with him. If he wants you to be there and represent him, he may only have to arrange it."

"Thanks," Ned said, "I'll pass that on. Will's preoccupied with his folks."

"Yeah, I get that," Lucca acknowledged. Ned nodded and moved toward his car. Lucca picked up the bags and walked toward the house as Ned drove away. Amelia stepped onto the porch, holding the door open for him as he climbed the stairs.

"Was that Ned's car leaving?" she asked curiously.

"It was. He had a question for me before he and Will drive to the coast tomorrow morning," Lucca replied, stepping inside the house.

Amelia stood in the doorway looking across to the castles, visible in the moonlight. She let her attention linger, wondering what would become of them. There was no way of knowing. Resigned to that truth, she turned and went back into the house.

* * *

Amelia was last to rise and dress in the morning, and could hear the chatter in the kitchen.

"Good morning everyone," she said as she joined them, finding Jasmine and Julia cooking breakfast. "Something smells delicious."

"Good morning," Jasmine said with a smile, looking up from buttering toast.

"I hope you're hungry," Julia stated, scooping scrambled eggs onto a serving platter.

Amelia moved toward David and Lucca seated at the table set for the meal. "I hope you two set the table," she said lightly as she sat down next to Lucca.

"Of course we did," David playfully declared. Lucca smiled.

"I'm surprised you're all up so early," Amelia noted.

"We're used to air conditioning," Lucca stated, "it's hard to sleep in the heat."

"How are we going to remedy that?" she asked with concern.

Lucca shrugged. "Swim lots and we'll be too tired to care. That's what I did as a kid."

"I remember that," Amelia said, smiling.

Jasmine and Julia brought platters with sausages, scrambled eggs, hash brown potatoes and toast to the table.

"Wow, that's a big breakfast on a hot day!" Lucca exclaimed.

"Julia's idea," Jasmine said. "Hungry mom breakfast".

"I'm very hungry," Julia stated and sat down. "Everyone dig in so I can start eating," she urged.

Amelia heard George's truck pull into the driveway, and excusing herself went out on the porch to meet him. He

E.G. Brook

climbed up the stairs, grinning at her.

"What are you grinning at?" she asked, finding it infectious and grinning herself.

"You're going to be a Grandma," he said, putting his arm around her waist as he reached her.

"Finally!" she exclaimed, laughing. "Come inside, Julia and Jasmine have made a big breakfast."

"Thanks, I've eaten. Coffee would be good."

"With cream."

"With cream," he said lightly, kissing the top of her head. He reached for the door and held it open for her, following her inside.

"Hey George," Lucca called, "maybe you can offer an unbiased view on something Julia and I are talking about."

"Hi everybody," George said, and turned to Lucca. "What's the topic?" Amelia indicated an available chair and he sat down. She brought him a mug of coffee and set it in front of him as he listened to Lucca, moving the cream within his reach.

"We're talking about the castles," Lucca said, "and whether it would be best for those living there to continue to live in them or move to another place. I think they ought to be able to keep living there, and Julia thinks moving to a newer place would be better."

Amelia sat between George and Lucca and began eating the breakfast someone had served for her. She watched for George's reaction.

"Sorry, I can't offer an unbiased view about the castles. I'm completely biased," he admitted.

"Mom?" Lucca asked.

"What's best is sometimes hard to determine," Amelia responded, and studied Lucca for a moment, wondering what was going on for him behind the question. "If it's a question of change or keeping things the same, I think change is hard for most people. It won't be any different for the friends in the castles. They've already been dealing with change this summer, we all have. The heat waves and Jack's passing have changed things, and the proposal for development has changed how we look at the castles. Whether they continue to live in the castles or move to another home, more changes are going to happen in their lives." She reached over and caressed Lucca's back. "I'd say what's best for them isn't a tangible thing Lucca. It's the love and care they have for each other. They'll keep that, whatever happens."

Lucca smiled. "Nailed it Mom, thanks."

David looked puzzled. Jasmine smiled.

Julia grinned. "Mom and Lucca have always had this behind the scenes way of communicating," she said to Jasmine. "David has yet to figure it out. It intrigues him." She rubbed her husband's back affectionately and he smiled, a little embarrassed. "We'd better get going," she said to him. "Ready?"

"Definitely," he said, standing up. Julia got up and began to clear their plates.

"Leave those Julia," Amelia said. "We'll clean up."

"Thanks," Julia responded, picking up her purse and walking with David to the door. "See you later at the lake," she called as they left.

"I'm going to take Jasmine for a tour of the vineyards, and then for lunch at the café," Lucca mentioned. "Would you two like to join us for lunch?"

Amelia looked at George, watching him as she spoke. "I'm thinking of stopping by the castles this morning to see how everyone's doing. Are you up for that George?"

George frowned. He held her gaze, recognizing she knew the challenge of what she asked. He resisted the temptation to turn away. "I can do that," he responded.

She smiled, reaching over and caressing his arm. She

turned to Lucca. "Let's meet at the lake around one, I'm not sure how long we'll be."

Lucca nodded, understanding the situation. He glanced at Jasmine whose expression gave him a sense she realized George had made a significant choice.

She smiled at him. "I'm ready to go to the vineyards after we clean up," she said. Lucca grinned and stood up, clearing the table with her.

Chapter 10

Amelia and George crossed the ball field without conversation. George was anxious about being at the castles with Jack gone. Amelia's thoughts were occupied with how to approach Nicia and the others about the possibility of a move. Only Emma had spoken at the meeting; she'd hoped they all would.

She automatically stopped at the outdoor tap by the edge of the orchard and pulled a scarf from her pocket, wet it, and tipped her head back so her hair hanging from the band holding it up fell away from her. She loosely tied the scarf around her neck.

"Water George?" she asked him. He shook his head no, pulling the brim of his hat forward to better shade his eyes. She pushed up her shirt sleeves, and splashed water on her arms and face, realizing she'd forgotten her hat.

They could hear Nicia talking as they neared the castles, and followed her voice into the backyard. Joe and Sarah were sitting in chairs next to her on her porch, and Emma and Merle were sitting on her steps. Sam, Phil and Hannah sat in chairs on Sam's porch, and Lucianna leaned against the porch railing. Ted and Ricco sat on Sam's steps.

Nicia greeted them cheerfully, "Hello you two."

"You're timing couldn't be better," Lucianna said. "We

were just talking about the meeting last night. How did you ever think of managing a crowd like that Amelia?"

"You mean facilitating the consultation?" Amelia asked, stopping by Nicia's porch. George walked on and sat next to Ricco.

"If that's what you call it," Lucianna acknowledged.

"I learned how. It's a process my grandfather attempted to teach me about when I was growing up, but I didn't really get it," Amelia replied. "I learned about it in a university debating class, of all places. The instructor introduced consultation as an experiment, and had the class use both consultation and debating in different scenarios, evaluating the results. I found consultation was the most effective, no question. I drew on what I remembered last night, though I might have been a little heavy handed."

George chuckled. Ricco glanced at him and grinned. "Well it worked," Ricco stated. "There were no shouting matches."

"I'd like to hear what each of you think about the possibility of things changing here," Amelia said, deciding to be direct.

"We have many thoughts," stated Lucianna, "but you own the houses Amelia. What's most important to you is what matters."

"Your thoughts are most important to me," Amelia said earnestly. "These are your homes."

Nicia spoke first, casually addressing them all. "I've lived here a long time, and when I ask myself if I could move now, at this stage of life, I think maybe now is easier than it might have been earlier. My husband has passed, my children are grown, it's just me to consider. I think maybe it's time to talk with my children about it. Maybe one of them will want to take me in, maybe more than one," she mused. She chuckled, adding, "Then I'd have to choose which place to go."

"I liked Will's idea of subsidized housing," Emma said,

"an apartment could be okay, I mean, we'd get used to it. Merle and I are pretty adaptable."

"To be honest," Ricco said, "I'd like to be able to stay here with my family. Lucianna and I have our two girls with us still, and this is our home. It's a good home, not with things newer homes have, but built well and with everything we need. It would be hard to move."

"We're guests here," Hannah commented, "but I've really appreciated how it is, everyone friendly, and helping each other out. I don't think that would be the same in an apartment building."

"Or maybe you'd find more friends," Nicia proposed.

"Maybe," Hannah acknowledged, "but that's not what I've experienced. Here, it's like everyone is family; good family."

"Sam, Ted, what do you think?" Amelia asked, walking toward them.

"I need subsidized housing," Sam stated. "I'm basically retired now, helping out in the vineyards when Ricco needs me, but not full-time work. I'd be okay to move if Will's apartments are subsidized."

"Same for me," Ted said. "Subsidized, great. Regular rent prices are out of reach." He pushed his hat back on his head a bit, looking down briefly and then out across the vegetable garden. "I don't know if an apartment would have the same space as the house though, that would be a problem," he added. "I have seasonal workers stay with me if they come from out of town, which means they can come."

Amelia gave him a puzzled look. "We have a house for seasonal workers from out-of-town."

"That's not enough for orchard and vineyard crews, and you've been housing both for years," Ricco said. "We only have a couple of year round guys who have their own places in town. We actually need more room for crew, not less."

"Suppose Quinn Orchards owned apartment units for each

of you and two additional units for crew. How would you feel about moving in that situation?" Amelia asked. No one responded. Merle looked out across the garden, and Lucianna looked at Ricco, who focused on the ground.

"We wouldn't have the garden," Merle said, "that would be the hardest part."

George turned from looking uneasily at Jack's house to Amelia. "Do you mind if I say something?" he asked.

"Please do George," she encouraged him, leaning against the railing near where he sat.

"What would be the reason for making the change?" he questioned. "Are the castles ready to be bulldozed because they're falling apart? Is more space needed for workers and the houses can't be upgraded to meet the need? Is it a financial issue, a lack of funds for upgrading, or a need to secure income from making a sale?"

Amelia looked from person to person. Everyone was silent.

Nicia frowned, considering what George had said. She turned to Amelia. "George asks an important question, what would be the reason for the change?" she asked. When Amelia didn't readily respond, Nicia added, "Maybe none of us knows. Maybe that question needs to be answered."

Lucianna spoke up. "You own the houses Amelia, it's for you to answer."

"Maybe money's the answer, because there's profit in it," Emma stated. "That would be true if you need or want to sell."

"It's not Amelia who has the need for money, it's Will," George said pointedly, challenging Amelia. "At first you were opposed to selling, and then you heard Will's father is sick and Will's supporting both his parents at the coast. He needs his developments to go ahead, and that's why you're considering selling."

Lucianna straightened up in astonishment. "Will's father is sick," she said to Amelia, "that's why you think of selling?"

"It's why I entered into a collaboration with Will and the town Council, to see if there could be a benefit to development," Amelia responded, remaining calm. She reached down and rubbed George's shoulder, letting him know she was okay with the challenge. He was tense.

"Will's need is important too," Nicia acknowledged, "so what's most important? That's a harder question to answer."

Ricco raised his head. "Make the change where it does the most good, that makes the most sense to me," he stated.

Amelia moved away from the railing, interested. "That could be developing the unused land," Amelia commented, looking to Ricco, "and leaving this land and housing as it is."

Lucianna looked at her with surprise. "Do you mean that?"

"I do," Amelia responded. "I can propose it at the Council meeting Wednesday. The decision will be made by the Council, Will and myself. I've agreed to that."

"Good," George said exuberantly, slapping his knee. "Let's talk about something else."

Lucianna laughed and patted him on the shoulder. "I'll get you something to drink," she said. "I'll get a drink for everyone." Ricco stood up to let her pass, and she walked down to their house, Hannah following her to help.

"Lucca mentioned he wants to be here for the harvest," Ricco said to Amelia. "It could be later than usual if the heat lingers."

"The weather could change suddenly once we get into September," Amelia noted. "Let's continue to plan for mid-month."

Ricco nodded. "His interest is growing," he added, "it's good to see. Alessandro would be happy."

Amelia smiled warmly. "He would," she agreed.

Amelia's phone rang and she pulled it out of her pocket,

checked the screen and answered the call. "Hi David," she said cheerfully, a slight frown coming to her face as she listened. "Well where are you? On the side of the road. Okay. Julia's going to be fine," she assured him, her frown easing into a smile as she guided David through his anxiousness. "Try this, get Julia to drive. Keep the air conditioning in the car on low, and if she feels nauseous again turn it off for a while and open the windows." She listened, still smiling. "Well this is the first pregnancy, there's lots to learn. Maybe take it slow this morning, relax a little. We'll see you at the lake this afternoon." She ended the call as Lucianna handed her a glass of iced tea.

"Thanks," she said, and took a long drink. As with all things Lucianna made, the iced tea was exceptionally good. "Does your daughter like working in the vineyards?" she asked.

"Oh yes," Lucianna responded, chuckling. "She's very happy to be working with her dad, and she loves to be outdoors. I think she was worried I'd be asking her to come work with me at the café."

Amelia smiled, appreciating the sentiment.

"Amelia," Nicia called, motioning for her to come. Amelia walked back to her porch.

"What is it Nicia?" she asked.

Nicia picked up a book from the small table beside her and held it toward Amelia. Her expression softened as she spoke. "Jack left this book to me that I thought you would like to have. It was your grandfather's."

Amelia put the glass she held on the table, feeling a warmth and familiarity with the book she couldn't explain. She took the book from Nicia, touched the cover and read the title, *The Promulgation of Universal Peace*. "I'm not sure if I've seen it before."

"Open it, there's an inscription inside."

Amelia opened the front cover and read her grandfather's handwriting on the inside page,

We pivot on relationships that endure, those that shape our lives, and those we're meant to build.
MQ

A shiver ran through her, she could remember him saying those words.

"Have you read it?" she quietly asked Nicia.

"Oh, yes," Nicia said. "Sometimes Jack and I would read it together. I remember when your grandfather gave it to him, so many years ago now." There was a hint of nostalgia in her voice.

Amelia heard George call her name. She looked up and saw him walking toward her with an uneasy expression. He indicated that he wanted to leave. Amelia nodded acknowledgement and turned her attention back to Nicia, handing her the book.

"If Jack left the book to you I'm sure he wanted you to have it," she said, affectionately caressing Nicia's arm. "Thank you for thinking of me."

Nicia sat back in her chair and held the book to her chest. She smiled and quietly assured Amelia, "Someday it will come to you."

With a quick goodbye to everyone, Amelia and George walked in silence from the castles. His effort to contain his emotions completely occupied him as they strode along the edge of the orchard and crossed the ball field. Amelia remained silent.

George could feel her compassion. He finally spoke as they crossed the dirt road in front of her home. "I felt like Jack was going to come out of his house and join us any minute," he said apologetically. "It got to be too much."

"It's okay, I understand," she assured him, gently placing

her hand on his back as they walked up the driveway.

"I'd like to have some time on our own before the others join us," he mentioned as they reached the top of the stairs. "Would you mind packing a lunch and going to the lake early?"

"That sounds wonderful," she responded warmly. "Wait here a moment while I get a few things."

"Sure," he agreed, and sat on the porch swing, rocking it gently back and forth.

* * *

It was late morning when they arrived at the lake. George set up a portable canopy by the trees to create more shade, unfolded a few chairs and left the cooler, bags and towels near them in his eagerness to get into the water.

Amelia was already swimming, almost at the dock. As she reached it she dove down and turned, heading back to shore refreshed by the coolness of deeper water. She stood when she touched sand on the shallow fringe of the lake, breathing heavily and feeling happy. Routinely loosening her wet clothing from where it clung, she lingered for a moment in the sun, watching George swim back from the dock. As he neared shore she turned and walked to the canopy, squeezing water from her hair before settling into a chair. She stretched her legs out in front of her, and closed her eyes. George soon flopped into the chair next to her.

"I don't know why we brought towels," he said, catching his breath. "Wait half a second and you're dry." He looked over at her peaceful expression. "Amelia?"

"No George," she calmly responded. "Let's not talk for a bit."

He got up and got himself a sandwich and bottle of water from the cooler, glancing at Amelia as he returned to his chair. He smiled. He never knew what to expect with her.

Smoothly unwrapping the sandwich he relaxed back in his chair, watching a paddler in a kayak as he ate. Amelia was still quiet, eyes closed, when he finished. "Are you sleeping?" he asked quietly.

Amelia chuckled lightly and opened her eyes. "Daydreaming," she replied. "Enjoying the peace." She sat up and reached over to the cooler beside her, taking out a sandwich and bottle of water. She unscrewed the cap on the water and took a drink, reminiscing as she looked out over the lake. "I used to relax like that when the kids were young and both so active," she said. "Sometimes I'd come here with Alessandro after he came in from the vineyard. He'd watch the kids and I'd just -" She swept her arm through the air in front of her, searching for a word.

"Zone out," George suggested.

Amelia smiled. "Get peaceful," she substituted. She took another drink of water. "Sometimes the pace of life moves faster than I do," she explained, "and I need to step off the path for a bit and let it move on by." She looked at George, wanting him to understand. "It took me a long time to learn that. Alessandro helped me," she stated. "Sometimes I think he understood me better than I understood myself." She smiled at him, unwrapped the sandwich and took a bite.

Emotional pain swelled in George, flushing into his face. He turned and looked out over the water, admitting to himself how much he wanted to feel peaceful. He lowered his eyes to the sand, pushing it around between his feet, wondering how long it would take to move through the grief of Jack's death; of Michael's death. He looked again to the lake, focusing on the sun sparkling on its surface, distracting himself from what he felt. He heard the cooler lid shut and turned, focusing his attention on Amelia. She stood watching him, and held his gaze for a moment. Her expression softened. She moved closer, crouching by his chair, reaching

E.G. Brook

up and lovingly sweeping his damp hair back from his brow.

"It takes as long as it takes," she said quietly.

"What does?" he asked, touching her cheek, caressing her soft skin, tracing her moist lips with his fingertips.

"Grief," she replied, and leaned toward him.

He closed his eyes, feeling the dampness of her kiss on his forehead. He wanted to lose himself in her. He opened his eyes and reached for her, holding her face in his hands, kissing her with a passion he hadn't allowed before.

"Whoa, George," she said, aroused by his kiss. He buried his face in her neck, kissing beneath her ear, sweeping his lips to her shoulder, his hands sliding down her back and around to her thighs. She reached for his hands, holding them tightly as she stood up and drew him up with her. She held him close.

"The pain will ease George, don't avoid it," she whispered. "Grief passes."

The sound of car tires on the gravel parking lot was unmistakable. George turned, seeing Lucca and Jasmine had arrived. He sighed and dropped his face into Amelia's hair, raised it and kissed the top of her head. They stepped back from their embrace, hands lingering briefly together. Amelia turned and waved as Lucca and Jasmine walked toward them.

George waved and chuckled, sitting back in his chair with a lighter mood. "Kids never seem to lose their timing," he said quietly. Amelia chuckled.

Jasmine reached the canopy and stopped next to Amelia, gazing out over the water. "Wow, the lake is beautiful," she said with awe.

"I hope you brought towels Mom, because I brought nothing," Lucca stated as he got closer.

"I have towels, but you probably won't need them," Amelia commented, turning her attention to Jasmine. "Did you enjoy the tour of the vineyards Jasmine?" she asked.

"Absolutely," Jasmine responded with a broad smile. "Lucca has told me so much about them in the last few weeks, it was wonderful to actually be walking through them. It's all so new to me."

Lucca took his shirt off, dropped it on the sand and ran toward the lake. "Come on in," he called to Jasmine as he splashed into the water.

"We just ate," she called back, being the voice of reason.

"Then wade or splash around," he laughed. "Just get wet and cool off." He dove in, swam out a few strokes and dove down under the surface.

"Come and sit down," Amelia said, moving into the shade of the canopy and getting a bottle of water from the cooler. She handed it to Jasmine, and motioned toward a chair as she sat next to George. Jasmine sat down, unscrewed the cap on the water and took a drink.

"You grew up in the city?" Amelia asked.

"Yes. This is my first small town, country experience," Jasmine replied, smiling. "It's pretty amazing."

Lucca joined them dripping from his swim. Amelia tossed him a towel and he dried himself off before flopping into a chair near Jasmine.

"We thought we'd stay for the week Mom, if that's okay," he said, still a little breathless.

"Sure. I'd love it," Amelia agreed.

Jasmine watched a couple of people on jet skis speed down the lake. "What a place to grow up," she said with amazement, turning to Lucca. "You're very fortunate. Do you know that?"

He smiled at her affectionately. "I know that," he responded, repeating her words. "And I've been realizing it more lately." Jasmine grinned and caressed his arm.

"How are you doing in the heat Jasmine?" Amelia asked,

E.G. Brook

handing Lucca a bottle of water.

"Thank you for asking. Lucca asks me the same thing, and I tell him I'm doing well. I'm very happy to be here." She smiled, looking at Lucca. "I especially enjoy the evening," she added. "I hope we can be outdoors again tonight."

"We definitely can," Lucca assured her.

They heard a car behind them and turned to see Julia parking, and getting out of the car with David. They both looked weary as they joined them.

"I'm ready to swim and relax," Julia said, sitting in the chair George set up for her and leaning back. "Actually I think we both are."

"Definitely," David agreed.

"Did you see any places you liked?" Lucca asked.

Julia wrinkled her nose. "Not really. It was a little discouraging."

"We have a week," David reminded her, "and there are more to see."

"True," Julia said, and sat forward. "I'm going to swim in my clothes to stay cooler longer," she stated, standing up and kicking off her shoes. "If that seems weird Jasmine, be forewarned."

George chuckled. "I'm sure your mother taught you that."

"She sure did," Lucca said, leaping up and racing Julia to the water, splashing her when she slowed to wade in. Amelia chuckled, watching them.

"Kids," David said, grinning. Amelia laughed.

"Oh David," she said, getting up, "you're in for such fun!" She moved quickly over the hot sand and into the water, passing Lucca and Julia splashing each other before they noticed her. She was swimming toward the dock when Lucca saw her and shouted, swimming after her.

Julia turned to David. "Are you coming in?" she called.

"In a minute," he called back to her.

Jasmine sat watching, smiling.

"Are you going in Jasmine?" George asked.

"Yes," she said, standing up and pulling her dress over her head, dropping it in the chair. She was wearing an attractive turquoise and black one piece bathing suit, and moved easily over the sand, diving into the water without hesitation. She swam very well, George noticed, and wondered if she had trained as an athlete. As he watched her climb onto the dock and join the others, he thought she was a good match for Lucca. Lucca was, as she'd said, very fortunate.

"There's just the two of us George," David said, tossing his shirt into Julia's chair. "Coming?"

"Well I can't be the old man on the shore," George joked, and walked with David down to the water, plunging in and welcoming the instant relief from the heat.

Chapter 11

The heat continued into the evening, cooling only slightly by the time they arrived at Amelia's home. Julia and David went into the backyard to plan the next day's house search, and Jasmine and Lucca went inside with Amelia to help prepare a light dinner. George relaxed on the porch swing, at Amelia's suggestion, endeavoring to stay awake as she came and went, bringing things to the coffee table for the meal. She offered him a glass of lemonade as she placed the pitcher on the table next to glasses, which he gratefully accepted. She was bringing out plates and cutlery when David stepped onto the porch.

"Julia's asleep in the hammock," he said, and sat in one of the wicker chairs.

"It's funny to see her tired and napping," Lucca said, coming from the house with bowls of salad. "Totally out of character for her." He set the bowls on the coffee table beside the plates and cutlery.

"Making babies is a lot of work, it takes energy," Amelia commented, holding the screen door open for Jasmine as she came out with plates of cold sliced turkey and ham. "You'd be amazed if you knew the details of what changes in a woman's body."

"What changes?" Lucca asked curiously, moving to sit on

the wicker sofa. Jasmine glanced at him as she passed, setting the meats next to the salads.

Amelia smiled. "Look it up Lucca," she teased, "you may need to know someday."

David chuckled.

"What's funny?" Lucca playfully challenged him.

"You being a dad would be totally out of character for you," David stated, laughing.

Lucca grinned. "True," he agreed, with a shrug of surrender.

Amelia chuckled and went into the house, returning with a plate of focaccia and setting it by the salads. "Help yourselves," she announced.

Jasmine began to dish food onto several plates, passing one to Amelia and taking one to George.

"Thank you Jasmine," Amelia said, appreciating the gesture. George smiled his thanks. Jasmine smiled in return, moving back to get the next plate of food as David finished dishing food onto his plate.

Julia sleepily reached the top of the stairs and joined them, sitting in the wicker chair by David. "Naps are fine," she said, "but waking up sleepy is weird."

"I'll get you something to eat," David said, setting his dinner down and picking up a plate for Julia. Jasmine handed him the salad tongs as she finished with them, taking her dinner and Lucca's and joining Lucca on the wicker sofa.

Amelia stepped over to Julia, holding her dinner in one hand and caressing Julia's shoulder with the other. "Hang in sweetheart, you'll figure things out," she assured her. "The sleepiness will pass. The move will come together when the time's right."

Julia looked up at her mom. "Did I not inherit the philosophical gene? I tend to think if it doesn't happen when I want it to, it's not going to happen."

Amelia chuckled. "That's not how it works baby."

David handed Julia a full plate of food. She smiled her thanks and blew him a kiss, picking up the fork to eat. She stopped and turned to Amelia, remembering she had information for her.

"Speaking of how it works," she said, "I found something online about your dream."

Amelia stopped eating, giving Julia her full attention. "Tell me."

"The words you saw written in a book actually exist in a book, *The Promulgation of Universal Peace*," Julia stated. Jasmine looked up from her dinner, listening attentively as Julia continued. "They come from a talk given at an open forum in San Francisco on October 10th 1912," she said, excited. "It's history Mom!"

"History?" Amelia repeated, astonished.

"I have that book," Jasmine mentioned with enthusiasm.

Amelia looked at her with surprise. "You do?"

"Yes, it's one of my favorites. My mother gave it to me as a gift."

Amelia suddenly recognized the title. "My grandfather had that book!" she exclaimed, turning to Julia. "Nicia showed it to me today. Jack left it to her."

"That explains it," Julia declared, her excitement subdued. "You probably read it when you were growing up, and now it's coming up in your dreams."

"I might have seen it in my grandfather's room," Amelia stated, "but I didn't read it. I don't know anything about it," she realized, wondering why it was associated with her dream. "Who gave the talk?" she asked.

"An older Persian man named Abbas Effendi, according to newspapers of the time," Julia said. "Those who knew him called him 'Abdu'l-Bahá. He travelled across the States in 1912 speaking to thousands of people, and even made a trip to Montreal. He was a big attraction. The book is a compilation of his talks."

Amelia still couldn't see a reason for the dream. "What was he talking about?" she asked Julia.

"Social issues. The newspaper articles I found referred to his emphasis on peace," Julia commented, "and I saw mention of equality of men and women, and overcoming prejudice. I didn't look extensively. I did notice he spoke about the threat of war in Europe, two years *before* the First World War. That intrigued me. He was really emphasizing the importance of achieving peace."

"But what I saw in my dream was about science," Amelia pointed out.

"I found the reference from your dream in the book, not the newspapers. Scanning through the talks I also saw mention of science and religion being harmonious and both important. That intrigued me too," Julia noted. She suddenly turned to Amelia in astonishment. "Maybe your grandfather met him Mom! Maybe that's what you're dreaming about."

Amelia was silent, feeling a sense of awe that her grandfather may have met the man. The image of her grandfather with the little girl came to mind. "But who's Grace?"

Julia shrugged. "I've no idea."

"Mom, Ned's pulling into the driveway," Lucca informed her, interrupting the conversation. Amelia turned, surprised to see Ned getting out of his car. She put her plate down on the coffee table and walked to the top of the stairs, taking the scarf from her hair that had loosened and was close to falling out. She put it in her pocket.

"Hi Ned," she called to him.

"Hello Mrs. Marin."

"Please call me Amelia," she requested.

"Amelia," he agreed. "Will's asked me to speak with you

tonight, are you available?"

Amelia glanced at the group, everyone indicated for her to go. "I am," she said, and quickly descended the stairs. "Let's go around to the garden at the back of the house. The family's just finishing dinner."

"Please lead the way," Ned said, stepping back so she could walk in front of him.

She led him to the chairs near the fountain and motioned for him to sit down. She sat opposite him and leaned back comfortably. "What's this about Ned?"

"Will won't be able to come back from the coast for the Wednesday meeting with the Council, his father's not doing well."

"I'm sorry to hear that," Amelia said with empathy. "I was hoping treatments were helping him."

Ned nodded in acknowledgement. "Will's planning to arrange for me to be at the meeting on his behalf, if possible. He also asked me to consult with you beforehand, to see if some agreements can be reached before the meeting. If we're successful, perhaps we can present our plans jointly to Council."

Amelia felt a little stunned by the turnaround in behavior, both Will's and Ned's. She wondered if it was genuine. "I'm surprised by the change in approach."

"Understandable. Will's acting with consideration of your preference for collaboration, and so am I," he emphasized. "His revisions are based on several factors, including the feedback from the community."

"Perhaps you could describe them to me," Amelia suggested.

"He's decided to let the Creek Road proposal go, and focus on the Quince Road project."

Amelia was astonished. "I came to the same decision."

"Good! That certainly indicates you and Will are coming

to common ground. Will's developed a plan for a diverse neighborhood on Quince Road. It would require rezoning from the permitted two acre lot size to one acre lots for single family homes, and further rezoning of three of those lots to accommodate townhouses. The focus of the development would be moderate middle-income housing rather than high end luxury homes. One townhouse complex would offer units for sale. The other two would offer subsidized rental accommodation, if the application for subsidized housing is approved."

Amelia commented with frank honesty, "Impressively thoughtful. Overall it sounds favorable to me."

"And specifically?"

"I've been considering sale of a portion of the 27 acres on Quince Road, while retaining a portion for donation to the town, and my personal use. Establishing a community garden was suggested at the public meeting and struck me as a very good idea. Approval to subdivide the land will be needed."

"What size parcels do you have in mind?"

"Twenty acres for sale and seven acres retained."

"Is there room to negotiate the size of the parcels?" Ned asked.

Amelia turned away for a moment, considering how flexible she was willing to be. "Perhaps," she decided, turning back to him.

Ned sat back in his chair.

Amelia smiled. "This is your favorite part isn't it? The negotiation."

Ned laughed in spite of himself, and his manner relaxed. "It is," he admitted, "and I feel confident you are an able participant."

"Make a suggestion," Amelia invited.

Ned sat thoughtfully for a moment, gazing across the garden. He turned back to Amelia and leaned forward, his hands clasped in front of him. He looked down at them, then up to Amelia. "Would you describe how you propose to use the seven acres of land, as you've mentioned donation to the town?"

"Three acres would remain natural habitat with trails for walking or cycling, and be a buffer between housing and the garden space. The community garden would be one and a half acres, accommodating small garden plots for individual or family use, and an additional half an acre would be planted as community orchard with a variety of fruit trees, perhaps a row of table grapes. The total five acres being donated to the town would depend on the Council's agreement to land use as I've described, as well as maintenance, and registry for community garden use. I'm considering two, one acre lots for personal use, which would require approval in subdivision as well."

Ned sat back with a faint smile, nodding in approval. "I like your plan. Would you consider reducing the area of natural habitat from three to two acres? There isn't a lot of natural vegetation up there, and I imagine trails will facilitate short strolls and viewpoint benches, small kids on bikes, things like that. Two acres could serve that purpose well."

Amelia smiled, acknowledging his point, yielding to the negotiation. "I'll agree to that. The land for sale will increase to 21 acres."

Ned stood enthusiastically. "Your plans are actually favorable for residents of the housing development. I have nothing better to offer. I'll talk with Will, and if he agrees with the size of acreage for sale, perhaps the two proposals could be presented jointly to Council."

"I'm willing to submit our proposals jointly," Amelia agreed, walking toward her front yard.

"Good. I'll pass that on to Will," Ned said, walking with her.

He turned to her as they reached his car. "I hope to see you in the meeting Wednesday. Thank you Amelia," he said sincerely, and extended his hand.

Amelia shook his hand warmly. "I'm glad we've found our way to agreement," she said. She watched him drive away, and shook her head in amazement at what they'd achieved. She smiled and headed to join her family on the porch.

Everyone turned to her expectantly as she reached the top of the stairs. She leaned against the porch railing and smiled. "We had an amazingly agreeable conversation. We're going to present our final proposals jointly to Council."

"Wow. Impressive," Lucca cheerfully declared. "What a change of focus for Will."

Amelia nodded, and her manner subdued. "Ned mentioned Will won't be back Wednesday. His father's not doing well."

Lucca's cheerful expression fell away, and he nodded acknowledgement. "I'll get in touch with him when I'm back home."

Amelia put her hand on his back and caressed it before she moved to the coffee table, picking up empty plates. She remembered how deeply Alessandro's illness had affected Lucca, and was glad he was willing to be there for Will.

George stepped forward to help clear the remnants of the meal, as did Jasmine. David got up and opened the screen door for them.

"I think everyone would like dessert," Julia said, getting up and following them inside. "Could I get that?"

Amelia stopped by the island. "I'm not sure what I have. Take a look in the freezer," she suggested. George started loading the dishwasher.

Julia opened the freezer and moved a few things around, then laughed. "You've got a tub of butterscotch ripple ice cream. I can't believe it!" she said as she pulled it out. "Dad loved this stuff."

"I remember," Amelia said, feeling a pang of nostalgia. "I still eat it sometimes." She took small bowls from the cupboard and set them on the counter next to Julia. "I found the tray," she added, pulling it out of a tall cupboard and setting it on the counter as Julia scooped ice cream. "I'd put it away with the others," she stated. "No idea why."

Julia chuckled, and arranged the bowls of ice cream on the tray with a handful of spoons. Amelia held the screen door open for her as she headed to the porch.

"Help yourself," Julia said, setting the tray on the coffee table. She took two bowls for David and herself, and returned to her chair. George came from the house and picked up a bowl, handing it to Amelia. He took one for himself and sat on the porch swing, patting the seat for Amelia to sit next to him. She smiled and sat down as Lucca took the last two bowls of ice cream for Jasmine and himself.

"Mom, could you take Jasmine and me on a tour of the orchards tomorrow morning?" Lucca asked.

"Sure," Amelia agreed. "Let's plan to go early."

Jasmine smiled. "Thank you, I'm eager to see them."

"David and I will be off early looking at houses again," Julia stated. "I hope it goes better than today."

Amelia turned to her. "I meant to suggest you try eating a smaller breakfast, and take several snacks with you. Maybe that will help the nausea."

"But I feel hungry all the time," Julia objected.

"If you can be back for lunch, even a late lunch, it would be a better time to eat a larger meal."

Julia sighed. "Okay, I hope it works."

Amelia got up and walked behind her, kissing the top of her head. "You'll be fine," she assured her. She put her empty bowl on the tray and walked to the railing, looking toward the castles in the twilight.

George stood up and returned his bowl to the tray, taking Amelia's hand and moving to the top of the stairs. "Time for me to head out," he said, and smiled. "Have a good night everyone."

Julia watched them go down the stairs and over to George's truck, talking briefly before George hugged Amelia and climbed into the cab. She leaned in the window and kissed him goodbye, stepped back and turned toward the house.

"What's going on with those two?" Julia asked.

Lucca was silent. Jasmine looked at him, puzzled, answering innocently, "They're in love."

Julia was shocked. "What?!"

Jasmine looked to each of them, feeling confused. "Didn't you know?"

Amelia reached the top of the stairs, and Julia looked at her accusingly as she stepped onto the porch.

"Mom could I talk with you inside for a minute?"

"Sure baby," Amelia said lightly, before noticing Julia's eyes were tearing up as she walked toward her. She stopped her, holding her shoulders and looking into her eyes. "What's wrong?" she asked with concern.

"Are you in love with George?" Julia blurted.

Amelia breathed deeply, knowing how possessive Julia was of those she loved. "I am," she said, looking straight into Julia's eyes, seeing a worried little girl in her grown daughter's face. "He's a wonderful man Julia, and he cares for us all very deeply," she reassured her. Tears streamed down Julia's face and Amelia held her close.

"But what about Dad?" Julia whispered, burying her face in Amelia's shoulder.

"I'll love him forever," Amelia said quietly, stroking Julia's hair and lifting her face up to look at her. "Love is abundant sweetheart. Loving George takes nothing away from my love for anyone else," she assured her. She wiped tears from Julia's cheeks with her fingertips, and smiled. "Okay?" she asked. Julia smiled weakly.

"David," Amelia called to him. "Would you please come and take your wife for a walk?" David got up and walked over to them, looking relieved. He put his arm around Julia's shoulders and they walked down the stairs. Amelia turned to Lucca and Jasmine.

"I'm sorry," Jasmine said with embarrassment. "I thought everyone knew."

Amelia smiled and caressed Jasmine's shoulder. "Don't be sorry Jasmine, I'm happy you acknowledged what you recognized. It needed to be said," she reassured her.

Lucca put his arm around Jasmine, she offered him a slight smile. He glanced into the yard and saw David and Julia walking across the ball field. "Julia's going to the castles," he noted.

Amelia looked in that direction, watching quietly for a moment. "Good," she said, feeling grateful. "Nicia and Sarah will help her." She lifted her hair back from her face and sighed. It had been another full day. She turned to Lucca and Jasmine apologetically. "Please excuse me you two, and enjoy the evening. I've got to revise the proposal to submit to the Council tomorrow."

"Go ahead Mom," Lucca said, standing up and taking Jasmine's hand. "I think we'll go for a walk." Jasmine stood and leaned into him affectionately.

"Good," Amelia said. She touched Jasmine's arm reassuringly as she moved toward the house. She paused in the doorway and turned back to them. "It looks like we could reach a unanimous decision at Wednesday's meeting." She chuckled. "Imagine!"

Lucca shook his head. "I never would have believed it. If Will's really shifted, we could have something to celebrate.

Let's meet at the café when it's over."

Amelia agreed with a grin, and headed inside.

* * *

The revision of the proposal took longer than Amelia expected. When finally finished she got herself another drink of water from the kitchen and returned to the bedroom feeling more than ready for sleep. She set the glass of water on the bedside table, and took the stack of papers from the printer. Tomorrow would be the day to sort and staple copies, she decided, and put the papers on her corner desk by the laptop computer.

She slid off her robe and tossed it over the rail of the footboard as she climbed under the sheet, her thoughts roaming to the events of the day. With a deep breath, she turned off the bedside lamp and laid down. Eyes closed, she focused on breathing, intending to clear her mind, not relive the day. She rolled onto her side, the faint night sounds in her room and outside the open window fading as she slid into sleep. The indistinct murmurs of her dream world became audible, and clear.

Jasmine's voice could be heard nearby. Amelia turned from where she stood picking cherries, and looked toward the castles. Beyond a broad shaft of sunlight she saw Jasmine, heavily pregnant, walking along the dirt road with Sarah. Her casual smile was radiant, the loose calf-length cotton dress she wore swayed with her movement. Sarah smiled and shifted the grocery bag she carried to her other arm, freeing her hand to caress Jasmine's growing belly before continuing to her home. Jasmine waved goodbye and walked toward Amelia.

"How are you doing Jasmine?" Amelia called.

"Fine," Jasmine replied, "moving a little slower." She reached the shaft of sunlight and turned toward it,

disappearing between the rows of cherry trees.

Amelia went to join her, but when she turned into the lane between the trees there was no sign of Jasmine. Sprinklers pulsed at the far end of the lane, and Amelia moved toward them. The sound of the sprinklers grew louder as she drew near, as if multiplying.

"Grandma," she heard a young voice say. Amelia turned and saw Grace standing behind her, just out of reach of water jetting from another set of sprinklers.

Grace smiled. "Can you show me now?" she asked.

Amelia knew exactly what Grace was talking about, and picked several dark red cherries from a tree, holding them before Grace's earnest gaze. "What do you think Grace, are they ready?" she asked. Grace took a cherry and put it in her mouth, chewing briefly before making a sour face and swallowing. Amelia laughed. "Your father used to do the same thing," she told her. "Maybe you were too little to remember what I showed you last summer."

She crouched down and held her hand with the two remaining cherries before Grace. "When you want to know if cherries are ripe, look at them carefully before you taste them," she said, examining one cherry and then the other. "Notice how big or small they are. Feel if they're soft or hard, roll them in your palm if you're not sure," she continued, doing what she described. "Smell them," Amelia encouraged, holding a cherry to Grace's nose, pausing while Grace sniffed, then replacing that cherry with the other. "If they smell slightly sweet, are soft to touch and look big and plump, rather than small and hard, go ahead and taste them," she said, smiling as she concluded, "These cherries are still quite small, they're hard, and they don't have much smell. They're not ready to eat."

"Let me try," Grace said enthusiastically. Amelia stood up and held a branch within Grace's reach while she picked a *few cherries.*

"What are you up to Mom?" Lucca teased as he joined them. "Developing the next generation of orchardists?" Jasmine walked up beside him in a loose summer dress.

Amelia smiled. "I'm just being Grandma," she responded, caressing Grace's hair.

Lucca chuckled. "Of course you are," he affirmed. He turned to Grace with a grin. "Maybe Grace won't be an orchardist, maybe she'll make excellent wines like her dad."

Grace laughed and ran over to him, hugging his legs. "That's not what Michael says. He says I'm going to help people make peace," she stated.

"Who's Michael sweetheart?" Amelia asked with curiosity.

Grace looked at Amelia with a frown. "You know him, he gave you the name Amelia. He took you where he lived."

Jasmine crouched down in front of Grace. "Do you mean Michael in your dreams?" she asked her daughter gently.

Grace hugged her mom happily. "Yes," she declared. She looked to Amelia, smiling confidently. "He's in Grandma's dreams too."

Grace went to Amelia, taking her hand and leading her further into the orchard. "Come and see," she insisted, but soon released Amelia's hand in her eagerness, and ran ahead.

Amelia lost sight of her, lost sight of the orchard, and emerged on the dirt road in front of her home. Her grandfather was there waiting for her, the young man Michael in a circa 1912 suit, leaning on the open gate to her driveway. He was looking down at the hat he twirled in his hands. "Grace," Amelia heard him say affectionately as she drew near. He raised his head, his face bright with confidence. "Soon," he proclaimed.

Amelia stirred in her sleep, rolling onto her back,

unconsciously sweeping strands of hair from her face. A breeze wafted in the window, lifting the sheer curtains with a breath of ease, refreshing the air. The curtains settled into stillness. Amelia smiled as she slept.

* * *

The morning air felt fresh to Amelia as she came into the kitchen with a vibrant smile. "Good morning," she said cheerily, taking a glass from the cupboard and stopping by the island counter to pour herself a drink of water. Jasmine and Lucca smiled from where they'd sleepily settled into chairs at the dining table. Julia and David sat opposite them, but were occupied with making plans for their day.

"You seem very cheery," Lucca noted.

"I slept through the night," Amelia stated with a broad smile. "It feels like the first time in months."

Julia turned to her. "What happened with the dream?"

"It evolved," Amelia replied, smiling. "And that's all I have to say."

"What?" Julia questioned, playfully taking the bait. "Are you not telling us something?"

"We'll all know when the time is right," Amelia prophesized. "At the moment we can move on with the day."

She grinned and turned her attention to Lucca. "I'm meeting with Ted this morning Lucca, but could visit wineries with you and Jasmine this afternoon if you're interested," she offered. "I'm curious to explore how they're doing, and you may want to taste their wines."

Lucca looked pleased. "That's a great idea," he said, noticing Jasmine's nod of agreement, "what time are you thinking?"

"How about right after lunch?" Amelia suggested. "I'll be home around 11."

"Okay," Lucca agreed. "We'll spend some time here this

morning, and make lunch."

"Maybe I'll try napping in the hammock," Jasmine said with a smile. "It worked for Julia."

"You're not sleeping?" Amelia asked, concerned.

"It's the heat Mom," Lucca responded. "It's keeping us both awake until it cools down in the early morning."

"Tonight we'll try ice and an extra fan in each of your rooms," Amelia stated. "It can help." She turned her attention to Julia and David. "How are you two doing?"

"Sleeping fine," Julia responded. "I think we're just too tired from the day to stay awake," she commented. "We've got another full day of looking at houses planned for today."

"And we should get going," David acknowledged.

"I'm ready," Julia stated, glancing to Amelia and anticipating her question. "We're going to pick up food and drinks from the café," she assured her.

Amelia smiled. "Enjoy the search," she encouraged. "Take your time with it."

Lucca got up and started making coffee as Julia and David left. "Did you get your proposal finished last night?" he asked Amelia.

"I did," she replied with an air of accomplishment, "and I'll be dropping it off this morning." She moved to a cupboard and took bowls, plates and mugs out for the three of them. "Only a few more days until the decisive meeting with the Council. I'm a little surprised by how eager I feel," she confided. "I hope it's a good sign."

"I have a good feeling about it," Jasmine stated confidently. "I'm looking forward to celebrating at the café."

Amelia poured glasses of water for Jasmine and Lucca and set them on the table. "Me too," she said enthusiastically.

* * *

Aria took water glasses from a tray and set them in front of Julia, David, and the other place settings on the table. Lucca and Jasmine arrived, weaving their way through customers, acknowledging Julia's indication for them to sit across from her and David. George smiled his greeting, listening to David describe a house he'd seen. Amelia burst into the café, spotted George standing beside David, and moved eagerly toward the table.

"What a meeting!" she declared. She stood by Julia, putting an anchoring hand on the back of her chair. "Council applauded the process we'd undertaken," she continued. "They even mentioned how community contributions assisted them. The Creek Road proposal was dropped. Our joint proposal for the Quince Road acreage was approved – re-zoning, subdivision, subsidized townhouses, trails and community garden – everything!" she stated with enthusiasm. "It was unanimous. Ned was close to exuberant when he expressed appreciation of the approvals on Will's behalf. He told us that with the funding granted for building subsidized housing, that part of the project will be developed first."

"That's incredible," Julia said, sitting back in awe.

Amelia laughed happily. "I'm so delighted!"

"Congrats Mom," Lucca said with a broad smile.

George grinned and nodded toward the other side of the room. Amelia turned and saw Ricco and Lucianna watching her. She lifted her arms in victory and shouted across the café, "The castles stay!"

Ricco hugged Lucianna and dashed out the door. Amelia laughed and sat down. George affectionately squeezed her shoulder and sat next to her. Amelia looked at Julia and David.

"Now I can finally tell you two I've kept an acre of land for you on Quince Road. It's yours if you'd like to build a home there," she said happily.

"Mom!" Julia gasped with surprise, and turned to David. "Build," she said, instantly enthusiastic. "We haven't even considered that as a possibility."

"No, but it's a great one," he responded eagerly. "And incredibly generous Amelia, thank you."

"How amazing!" Julia exclaimed.

"Drive by tomorrow and see how you feel about the area," Amelia suggested, reaching for her glass and taking a drink of water.

"Come with us," Julia insisted. "All of you come with us," she declared happily.

"I'd love to, but George is working," Amelia said, turning to George. "Any flexibility in your day tomorrow?"

"Name the time and I'll be there," he agreed.

"Great, let's make it at nine," Julia acknowledged enthusiastically. "Lucca and Jasmine?" she asked, turning to them.

Lucca looked at Jasmine, she nodded yes. "We're in," he stated. He turned to Amelia, "So Mom," he teased, "does this mean I get land to build on if I move back here?"

Amelia smiled playfully and lifted her hair back from her face. "Try me," she baited him.

* * *

A refreshing breeze wafted over the hillside as they arrived at the Quince Road acreage the next morning. A promise of cooler temperatures to come, Amelia hoped as they walked onto the land. The breeze blew wisps of hair about her face as she pointed out the plot of land to Julia and David, and she reached up and kept it from her eyes. She watched the two of them wander over the acre, checking different possibilities for a building site, turning to the view each time. David was increasingly excited by the thought of designing their home.

E.G. Brook

Julia was ecstatic.

"I'm so amazed this is happening," Julia admitted, hugging Amelia close.

"Me too baby," Amelia whispered into her daughter's hair.

"Julia come and check this out," David called. Julia stepped back, looking toward him, wiping her eyes with the back of her hand as she smiled.

"Go ahead," Amelia encouraged, caressing her back.

Amelia looked for the others as Julia moved across the grass to where David was standing. She noticed Lucca and Jasmine had walked farther up the hillside, and seemed to be in deep conversation. George had wandered off on his own, and stood mesmerized by the view of the valley and distant lake.

"I've never seen it from up here before," he said, putting his arm around her as she walked up to him. "It's beautiful."

She wrapped her arm around his waist, moving into the pleasure of his closeness. A fleeting thought came to her and she looked up at him, briefly wondering what would come of their relationship. His face was bright, his expression open as he gazed over the valley.

"You look very happy," she commented quietly.

He looked down at her with an unexpected tenderness. "I'm feeling a lot of things," he confided, a vulnerability in his eyes she'd never seen before. "We can talk about it another time," he promised, and kissed the top of her head.

Amelia smiled. "I'm not sure if I ought to plan to wait for that, or look forward to it," she said honestly.

"Look forward to it," he said, his eyes smiling.

*

E.G. Brook

egbrook.com